The Kruger Mines wanted profits at any cost!

● The big hydraulic pumps shot a continuous jet stream of water into the virgin hills. Huge sections of mountainside quivered under the impact and dissolved into a torrent of mud. In the valley below, the once-green pastures disappeared and cattle died of thirst and starvation. The ranchers grew desperate.

● With their homes at stake, a courageous group banded together to fight Kruger with his own methods. Soon the night resounded with the thunder of hoofbeats as the ranchers rode to win back their way of life.

THE NIGHT RIDERS

was originally published by
Doubleday & Company, Inc.

Are there paperbound books you want but cannot find at your retail stores? pb

You can get any title that is in print in these famous series:
POCKET BOOK EDITIONS • CARDINAL EDITIONS • PERMABOOK EDITIONS
THE POCKET LIBRARY • WASHINGTON SQUARE PRESS • ALL SAINTS PRESS
Simply enclose retail price plus 5¢ per book for mailing costs.
Do not send cash—please send
check or money order to............Mail Service Department
                                            Pocket Books, Inc.
                                            1 West 39th Street
Free catalogue sent on request   New York 18, New York

THE NIGHT RIDERS

Todhunter Ballard

A POCKET BOOK EDITION published by
POCKET BOOKS, INC. · NEW YORK

THE NIGHT RIDERS

Doubleday edition published March, 1961
Pocket Book edition published March, 1963
1st printing..........January, 1963

All of the characters in this book
are fictitious, and any resemblance
to actual persons, living or dead,
is purely coincidental.

This original *Pocket Book*** edition is printed from brand-new plates made from newly set, clear, easy-to-read type.
Pocket Book editions are published by Pocket Books, Inc., and are printed and distributed in the U.S.A. by Affiliated Publishers, a division of Pocket Books, Inc., 630 Fifth Avenue, New York 20, N.Y.
*Trademark registered in the United States and other countries.
**Trademark of Pocket Books, Inc., 630 Fifth
Avenue, New York 20, N.Y., in the United States
and other countries.

L

Copyright, ©, 1961, by Todhunter Ballard. All rights reserved. This *Pocket Book* edition is published by arrangement with Doubleday & Company, Inc.
Printed in the U.S.A.

The Night Riders

CHAPTER ONE

CELL BLOCK NINE was quiet under the early dark of the November evening. The rough walls of hewn stone bled their moisture, adding dampness to the chill of the foul air.

The bracket lamp in the corridor struck a finger of light through the small grilled peep window in the heavy plank door.

Mitch Barton shivered and squinted through the light at his cellmate. Kid Boyd had caught up a shoe and hurled it at a rat, cursing in his soft voice.

This was like any other night in the block. Barton had seen many of them, over three thousand six hundred, for he had been behind the gray prison walls nearly ten years now.

And yet it was not like any other night, for there was a rising excitement within him, an anticipation such as he had not experienced in a long while.

He spoke to Boyd in a low, controlled voice. "You might as well try to sleep. It won't be before midnight."

They both understood why. The guard who only last week had managed to be shifted to block nine would not come on duty until twelve.

The prison was noted as one of the hardest to break out of, but when you had a guard who had taken his job for the sole reason of freeing you, your chances were better than even. It was a careful plan. It had taken nearly two years to formulate.

Mitch Barton stretched his six-foot bulk on the narrow bed, feeling the network of laced springs through the thin husk mattress. He closed his eyes but sleep would not come.

He forced himself to lie, not moving in the half-darkness, hearing the tramp of the guard's feet along the passage, sensing rather than seeing the man pause, peer into their cell, then move on.

Time dragged. Time usually meant nothing here, for there was nothing to wait for, but tonight his impatience gave it chains. He tried to imagine how it would be to ride a horse again, to feel the wind on his face, the heat of the sun, the cooling touch of rain.

Strange, the little things a man missed, cooped behind the walls, the natural things of which he had thought nothing before the doors had closed upon him.

He drifted into a state near hypnosis, awake yet not awake, so that when the key finally clicked in the door's lock he sat up with a start.

The guard's name was Powers. He had been a small rancher in the north end of the valley, but Mitch had not known him before. Now he greeted him as a close friend, knowing well the sacrifices Powers had willingly endured to make this night possible.

Two years of service in the prison before finally securing the transfer to block nine. For block nine held the most desperate inmates, and those whom powerful forces outside the walls wished closely guarded. Powers was told of the cost before he took the job, warned by the man who had set up the plan, who had himself spent five years in Folsom and knew everything there was to know about the place.

He whispered now as Barton and Kid Boyd came off their bunks.

"Steady. I'll have to walk you out one at a time, as if you're headed for death row. If any of the rest along the alley get the idea there's a break..."

"What about Clyde Miller? He's three cells down."

Powers groaned. "He's in with Rankin. If we take him we'll have to take Rankin too."

Rankin was a convicted murderer.

"Take him," said Barton. "I'd take the devil himself before I left Clyde in this hole."

Powers nodded. He pulled a revolver from his waistband and handed it to Boyd. He found a second gun and pressed it into Barton's grasp.

Then, motioning Boyd to follow him, he moved silently back into the corridor.

Barton waited just inside the door. Ten years before he had not been a man of violence. He had even condemned the other ranchers who had blown up the flumes and cut the mining company's water ditches. But Folsom had hardened him and he knew that rather than face another fifteen years in the narrow cell he would die in this attempt to escape.

There was no hope of pardon for him. The mining men who had packed the jury, who had railroaded him, were still as powerful as any in the state. They controlled the legislature, the courts, the elected county officials. And they feared Barton as they feared no one else.

He stood tense, the gun held under the lower edge of the striped prison jacket, until he heard the scuff of the guard's heavy shoes on the rough stones. Then as Powers stopped he slipped through the door, moving ahead of him along the passage quietly, not so hurried as to attract the interest of any convict who might be peering out of the grilled window of his cell door.

They reached the corridor's end without incident, and Barton stepped through the door which separated the block from the main portion of the prison.

Powers went back again. Barton and Boyd waited, their guns ready, their senses sharp.

Kid Boyd was thin and very tall. He towered over Barton by five inches. His face was narrow, nearly chinless, his hands so large that the .44 he now held was fully concealed.

But his voice was high, almost squeaky, and even after years of living in close proximity to the man it still startled Barton that such a high-register sound could come from so big a chest.

"Think we'll make it?"

4 / THE NIGHT RIDERS

There was a desperate urgency behind the words as if Boyd refused to trust himself to believe that they actually had a chance.

"We'll make it."

Barton saw Clyde Miller come from his cell and move toward them with a tread made heavy by advancing age. He reached them, gripping Barton's arm wordlessly. His blue eyes, no longer keen as they once had been, showed the glint of tears.

Powers went back once more and reappeared a moment later with Rankin before him. Rankin was in his mid-thirties. His hair was a sandy red, his blue-green eyes squinty as if he had looked too often into the sun.

He grinned crookedly, saying nothing, as unconcerned as if he had known of the planned escape from the first.

Wordlessly they turned along the outer corridor toward the guard room at the end. Powers walked in front, Boyd and Barton directly behind with their guns, Rankin and Miller at the rear.

There was one guard in the room, reading an old newspaper by the glow of a student lamp. As they came against the bars he looked up, and his mouth dropped open as he saw the gun in Powers' hand pointing directly at his chest.

"Get on your feet."

The guard rose slowly. "You out of your mind?"

He was covered now not only by Powers but by Boyd and Barton. Barton took the lead unconsciously.

"Get the keys. Come over and open the door if you want to live."

The man moved slowly, lifting down the ring of heavy keys from its place above the desk and coming forward to turn the huge lock. They were through the door at once, Barton spinning to lift the guard's gun from its holster and toss it to Rankin who caught it expertly.

"Now strip."

The guard pulled off his uniform. Barton, nearest his size,

peeled out of his prison stripes and donned the thick blue trousers and brass-buttoned coat. The flat, hard cap was small, but he thrust it to the back of his head.

"Tie him up."

"Hell with it."

Before they could guess his intention Rankin stepped forward and swung the guard's own gun against the uncovered head, hard. The man went over without sound, falling to the bare floor.

Barton said harshly, "Why did you do that?"

Rankin sneered at him. "What did you want me to do, kiss him? He dumped me in solitary twice."

Barton caught the lighter man's shoulder and swung him around.

"Let's get one thing straight, you and me. The only reason we brought you was to get Miller out. If you ever try anything without my orders I'll kill you."

Fred Rankin looked at him. It seemed to Barton that the green eyes mocked him, the thin-lipped smile held insolence, but he had no time to waste now.

"Come on. Let's move."

They filed out through the guard-room door, into the paved square. There were three other men within this prison whom Barton would have liked to liberate, but they were in other cell blocks. There was no chance. They moved slowly, toward the main gate, following the wall. There was no moon. They had chosen this night purposely. They reached the guard house without alerting the men on the walls above, and Powers slipped through the door.

Two men were on duty inside, playing pinochle, relaxed. They looked up in surprise as Powers came in.

"What are you doing out of the block?"

"It's Curtiss," he said, naming the man Rankin had hit. "I've got to have help."

They stared at him. The sergeant in charge climbed to his feet.

6 / THE NIGHT RIDERS

"What's wrong with him?"

"He's having some kind of a fit."

The sergeant turned to the door. As he passed through it Barton shoved his gun against the man's side.

"One sound and you're dead."

The sergeant froze. Powers had not followed. Powers was covering the remaining guard. The man half-reached for the cord of the alarm bell. Powers knocked his arm aside. Deliberately, with none of Rankin's viciousness, he laid the barrel of his gun alongside the guard's head.

They were free. Even Barton could not quite believe it. It had gone without a hitch. They slid through the wicket in the big gate, ghosted across the dark ground. Five minutes later they reached the horses. Barton was relieved to see that Carl Dill and Emmett Foster had brought extra mounts. He had been worried that with Miller and Rankin added to the escape party they would be short.

No one hurried. They walked the horses, heading along the river, Barton and Emmett Foster in the lead, seven men riding quietly through the night.

The only thing which would have attracted attention was that two wore the uniform of prison guards, three the striped suits of convicts.

Five miles.

In a small grove against the river they halted, turning deep into the protection of the trees. Foster had brought extra clothing also. A good man, Emmett. He had been one of the original Night Riders, one who had escaped the trial. It was to him that Barton had sent Carl Dill on Dill's release from the prison.

Clyde Miller was crying softly to himself, shedding his striped suit and fumbling into the nondescript butternut pants, the worn brown shirt. Kid Boyd was unusually silent, Rankin watchful, a few paces apart. Barton finished his dressing and extended his hand to Powers.

"I won't even try to thank you."

The ex-prison guard was embarrassed. He said in a studied voice, "I didn't do it for you. I did it for the valley. You're the only man the Night Riders will follow. We've been starving and I don't like to starve."

Barton turned away, his eyes falling upon Rankin beside his horse.

"Good luck."

The murderer lifted his head. "Meaning you want me to ride out?"

"You aren't one of us. There's nothing for you here."

"I got no place to go."

Barton hesitated. He did not trust Rankin, his violent temper, his killer instinct. But ten years in prison had taught him realities. They were in a fight, outweighed in both numbers and money. It was all right to put a bunch of ranchers onto horses, to call them Night Riders, to set out to attack the largest mining combination the country had ever seen if all they wanted was adventure. But if they really hoped to succeed they needed professionals, men who knew how to use a gun against men, who would match the killers on the other side.

"Your choice," he said briefly, and turned to Kid Boyd. "Bury those uniforms so they won't be found."

Then Barton touched Carl Dill's arm and moved off, up the river bank. He wanted a careful, uninterrupted report from Dill on the conditions in the valley.

They squatted on their heels in the deep mud and Dill found a cigar in his breast pocket, passing it over silently. He too knew the agony of going for weeks, sometimes months without the solace of tobacco.

Mitchell Barton drew in the fragrance deeply, letting the smoke lie warm and soothing in his throat for a moment before he exhaled.

Through the gloom he could not see the man beside him clearly but he knew him thoroughly. For his first five years in prison, they had shared a cell.

Carl Dill was neither a rancher nor a valley man. He had

8 / THE NIGHT RIDERS

been the auditor for the mining syndicate, and he had stolen fifty thousand dollars of the syndicate's money. He had done time for the theft.

The one thing they had in common was their hatred. Both hated Donald Kruger. It had drawn them together, and since his release from prison Dill had worked tirelessly to effect this night's escape.

He said now, "I've got the perfect headquarters set up. The old Haskell mine."

Mitch Barton knew the place. Twenty years before a group of Easterners had bought out the Haskell claims in the rocky hills south of Grass Valley. They had spent a million dollars, carving in a road, putting up buildings, drilling their haulage tunnel. Then the vein had petered out and the whole project had been abandoned.

"The road's washed badly," said Dill, "but there's a trail you can get over with a horse. A company of cavalry couldn't come in there if two men were guarding that trail."

Barton nodded. "How do the valley people feel?"

"As mad as ever. But Kruger's men keep them off balance, and they don't trust me. I'm an outsider. When they learn you're in the hills though, they'll rally, don't worry about that."

Barton waited for a long moment, then asked the question which lay always uppermost in his mind.

"My boy. Did you find him?"

Dill was silent as if he hated to answer, and Barton had a cold, sick feeling of apprehension.

"He's in Morgan's Ferry."

Barton half-straightened in surprise.

"What's he doing there?"

Again Dill hesitated. "Dealing faro."

"Dealing faro? How come?"

"Your sister-in-law has the faro bank in Cap Ayres' saloon."

Barton cursed under his breath. After another long pause he asked, "How many people know who they are?"

"Everyone. Your cousin Finley saw to that. He's quite a rat, you know. He sold out to Kruger's men. He's informed them of everything you've ever written him. He wants your ranch."

Barton stood up. He said tensely, "All right. Let's go get the boy."

Dill had come up also. "I was afraid of this. I almost didn't tell you."

"If you hadn't I'd have killed you."

Dill's voice tightened. "But you can't ride into the Ferry. That's what they'll expect you to do. They'll be there waiting for you. I understand how you feel about the child. . . ."

"The hell you do." Barton's voice was rougher than Dill had ever heard it. "I never saw him. My wife died in childbirth after I was sent away.

"I can't leave him there. Donald Kruger would like nothing better than to hold him as hostage, and I wouldn't entrust a snake to his tender care. I've got to get the boy. Let's ride."

CHAPTER TWO

BARTON'S MEN CUT the telegraph wires in half a dozen places, carrying away whole sections to make repairs more difficult. It was over an hour before their escape was discovered, but still the news that Barton was free flashed across the central portion of the state.

It reached Donald Kruger in his massive home in Burlingame. It reached the mines at North San Juan and Bloomfield. It brought men out of bed and sent them into hurried conferences.

For everyone involved knew that the whole valley was a

10 / **THE NIGHT RIDERS**

powder keg, and Mitchell Barton the fuse which could send it into explosive violence.

Creighton Hague sat in his office above the Ione pit. The office was of logs, four rooms, each heated by an iron stove. The building was dwarfed by the scene outside. There a dozen giant monitors played their seventy-five-foot jets of water against the huge seam of tertiary gravel which was the mountainside.

The gravel was the bed of an ancient river, buckled in some prehistoric upheaval of earth. It was partially cemented by ages and pressure, yet it crumpled before the onslaught of the powerful streams, the force of a thousand fire hoses, and with the gold it held washed down through the long sluices. A million dollars' of gold a month. A million tons of rock and soil and brush.

The monitors ran twenty-four hours each day. Their roar, like the swelling volume of a hundred tornadoes could be heard for miles. Hague, like all who worked near the pits, was partly deafened from the constant assault against his eardrums.

He was a big man, wearing a neat flannel shirt against the cold foothill air. Fat showed in loose rolls beneath the shirt. Ten years older than Mitch Barton, he had clawed his way up from mucker in the pits to manager of the operation.

He was proud of his accomplishments, proud of his job, proud that Donald Kruger and his associates trusted him. He lived and breathed for the mining company.

No man could have reached his spot nor held it without being ruthless, and Hague had made a virtue of ruthlessness all of his life.

There came a ghost of noise at the office door and Hague swung to see Kodyke in the entrance from the outer room. Hague had never accustomed himself to Kodyke. The man was tall, thin, with a narrow face and a too-large nose. The eyes always held Hague, eyes of a dead man, lidless as a lizard's, with the fixed intensity of a cobra. Even Hague was repelled by the machinelike deadliness that was Kodyke.

THE NIGHT RIDERS / 11

He knew nothing about the man's history. Kodyke had appeared at the mine one day bearing a letter from Kruger. Kodyke was to head the dread company police. He ran the change rooms. He threw out the hi-graders. He supervised the cleanups and handled the shipments of raw gold which each week went out to San Francisco.

Hague squeezed down his uneasy dislike. He pulled open the top drawer of his desk and drew out a tintype.

"This is Mitchell Barton. He broke out of Folsom last night. Apparently he bribed one of the guards. We want him back there or we want him dead."

Kodyke took the picture in a lean hand, studying it thoughtfully.

"Dangerous?"

"Dangerous, yes. You know how the ranchers in the valley are. They blame us for all their troubles. Ten years ago they blew up some of our ditches. It cost us a hundred thousand dollars and thirty days lost time to fix them. We don't want Barton's Night Riders loose again."

The gunman nodded, slipping the picture into his breast pocket, saying nothing.

Normally Hague wasted no words, but now he found himself unable to stop their flow although he knew Kodyke was aware of all he said.

"His son is in Morgan's Ferry. His sister-in-law is a gambler. They call her the Yankee Duchess. She has the faro bank at Cap Ayres' saloon . . ."

Kodyke cut in, cut Hague short. "Is Barton alone?"

Hague shook his head, pulling a map from the drawer.

"I don't know how many are with him. Four escaped from the prison. The guard went along. How many were waiting outside with horses is hard to tell. But it will take them twenty-four hours to make the Ferry. You can be there before that."

"You think he'll try to see the boy?"

"Knowing Barton I think he will," Hague said.

Kodyke nodded again, turned without further orders and left

12 / THE NIGHT RIDERS

the room. Under the gunman's silence Hague heard the echo of his own garrulousness and was irritated with himself.

Kodyke had heard only what he needed. Already his mind was busy with plans as he headed toward the bunkhouse and his crew. He knew the temper of the valley. He had watched the hatred on the people's faces as he and his police rode through their towns, and he had his spies. Being the man he was he had a deep and abiding belief that anyone in this world could be bought if the price was right.

He had dealt with Finley Barton, Mitch's cousin, and he felt certain that Finley had not known of the proposed escape. Had he known, he would have warned them. He folded the map, fitting it to his pocket, and considered what effect Barton's freedom would have on Donald Kruger.

Of all the employees of the wide-flung mining operations Kodyke was aware that he knew Kruger best. Little went on around Alf Kodyke that he missed. He had had to be on his guard to survive.

He had been only sixteen when he had killed his first man. That had been in the Nations, the spawning ground for so many of the outlaws who had been roaming the country since the Civil War.

He had fled northward from the Territory to the Kansas cow towns, and under another name had killed three men in Ellsworth before he turned westward.

Kruger had seen him shoot the gun from another's hand in a San Francisco bar, had secured his release from jail and offered him a job. Kodyke had never asked why he was chosen. He only knew that Donald Kruger had been the only man in his life to do him a favor.

In return Kodyke gave him full loyalty, but not blind loyalty. The gunman had little education but a shrewd, native comprehension. He had spent months as Kruger's bodyguard, taking the mining king home when he was drunk, mothering him in his fits of mental depression, watching and learning.

Kodyke meant to cash in on his patron's position and he

meant that nothing would happen here in the valley to jeopardize that position. Barton had to be found and killed.

He roused ten men. He led them to the corral for horses and then turned down the winding trail, the short cut to the Yuba.

Outside of the town he halted, showing his crew Barton's picture and giving his instructions carefully. They were to guard the roads. They were not to bother anyone entering, but they were to hold anyone leaving who might by any possibility be of Barton's party.

Then alone he rode boldly in through the late-afternoon sunlight. He had to learn whether Barton had already come and gone, for if the Night Riders had quit the Ferry he wanted to be on their trail as rapidly as possible.

Alone, he felt that he would not attract too much attention. He was a fairly regular visitor in all the cattle towns of the region, and he rode with a contempt for the muttered threats of the ruined ranchers whom he knew would be pleased to kill him.

He left his horse at the rail before the Oriental Saloon and came through the door, finding the place only partly filled. The room was large and had once been ornate, for at its height Morgan's Ferry had been one of the biggest gold camps along the Yuba.

But the time was gone when a man could pan his ounce a day from the stream, and the town now lived only on the lessening trade from the surrounding ranches.

The Oriental like the rest of the dowdy buildings was already old, its glory shadowed, its plaster cracked and soiled. Even the huge painting of the nude that hung like an offensive gargoyle above the bar was wounded below the left breast where a flying bottle had struck the canvas.

But Kodyke had no interest in the picture, or in the room. His eyes went to the faro bank and he saw with relief that the game was being dealt by a ten-year-old child.

He leaned against the far end of the bar, watching as the

14 / THE NIGHT RIDERS

boy's small hand lifted one card and then another from the *shoe*.

There was no change of expression on the young face, no sign of feeling. He had been carefully schooled, this ten-year-old son of Mitch Barton, this youngster whom gamblers called the Tiger.

But even his interest in the boy was fleeting. His attention turned to the woman who stood at the child's side.

The Yankee Duchess, men called her, and there was not a better-known gambler on the Pacific Coast. Before she reached twenty she had been running the fashionable gaming rooms of the lavish Murmont Hotel in San Francisco.

These rooms had already been operated for nearly twenty years by her father, Harry Beauchamp, and the daughter had carried on after his death.

Kodyke knew all about her and her history, and how she had raised her younger sister Lucy. He stood studying Marie Beauchamp now. He knew she hated Barton as thoroughly as did Kruger. He debated speaking to her, asking her help in trapping Barton and the convicts with him, and decided against the move as unnecessary.

But his interest in the woman lingered. Few women in his experience had held Kodyke for long, although he had been well known in the sporting districts of the Kansas cow towns.

He was too self-controlled to entrust anyone, even a woman as attractive as the Yankee Duchess, with close relationship. But he admitted to himself that she would be pleasant to have, and he filed the thought for future reference, for a time when he was not pressed by more important business.

Kodyke turned and moved quietly from the saloon, not aware that Cap Ayres had observed him through the peephole in the wall beside the backbar, the peephole which enabled Ayres to know what went on in his saloon without his leaving his private office.

CHAPTER THREE

THEY RODE TOWARD ROSEVILLE, swinging north before they reached the town. Daylight came. Still Barton pressed on, using back trails and lightly traveled roads.

The signs of desolation grew as they progressed, but it was not until they reached the Yuba that the extent of the havoc wrought upon the land by the hydraulic mines was fully evident.

The crystal-clear river Barton remembered now seeped coffee-colored water, soup thick, through a maze of mud banks and choking bars, a scattered waste clogged with rocks, with broken trees which blocked the once-free channel.

At the moment the stream was scarcely two feet deep, fighting its way to its juncture with the Sacramento and American, thence to carry its destroying flotsam to nearly fill the harbor at San Francisco.

Barton knew from bitter experience that cattle would die of thirst rather than drink the polluted stream, that many of them had swallowed so much sand it had killed them.

But even the low water was not the worst. It was at flood time that the main damage was done. In spring the snow-fed rivers rose, overflowed their littered channels to inundate millions of acres of grass beneath the cloying silt. These floods season after season drowned livestock, carried away homes and built the rubble carpet ever higher, multiplying the blight until nothing but wild oats would grow on the caked, cracked surface.

Once he had believed that reason, that law could prevail, that there was no need for violence. He had argued and worked for an anti-debris law which would force the mining company to build check dams, to store the water from their flumes until the solids settled from it.

He had been in San Francisco seeking an interview with Donald Kruger when his neighbors, the ranchers, had blown up the water ditches. But it had saved him nothing. He still had gone to prison.

He edged his horse forward carefully into the caking mud, feeling the animal sink in the sludge, feeling it jump in sudden panic as the suction threatened to pull it under.

He spurred. They lunged on, and somehow the horse managed to struggle through, to lurch up the far bank and stand quaking in its fear.

Barton turned to watch his fellows as one by one they made the crossing. Clyde Miller's horse went down, throwing the old man clear but thrashing until it was dangerously mired.

Barton loosened the rope from his saddle, wondering if after ten years he could still build a loop. It took him two casts before the noose fell across Miller's shoulders. The man worked it down, under his armpits, and they snaked him free, working him gradually from the holding mud so not to break his legs.

Once free he slid toward them as if the brownish sand was so much grease.

The horse was a different matter. It writhed in terror, half on its side, trying doggedly for a foothold in the yielding bog.

Barton put a rope around its neck but it was already sunk too deeply. He stood a moment on the bank, regretting what he had to do. Then slowly he pulled the revolver from his belt and put two bullets into the animal's head.

Afterward, using the rope which his well-trained mount held taut, he worked back into the stream to recover the rifle and saddle.

At the first ranch beyond the river Carl Dill rode off to buy a fresh horse while the men stayed concealed in the brush a mile away. As they waited, cleaning the sticky slime from their clothes and from the horses, Barton swore.

"I'd forgotten how bad it is."

Emmett Foster said in his slow drawl, "You haven't seen the worst. At Marysville the cherry orchards are buried under twelve feet of the stuff. This used to be the prettiest stretch of country the Lord ever made. Another five years and it will be nothing but wasteland."

"It won't go on for another five years." Barton's face was tight. "I don't know how much Dill has told you about Kruger and his operations . . ."

Foster shook his head. "It's hard to believe."

He was a quiet man, middle-aged, solid, and unimaginative. He owned the ranch north of Barton's and Barton had known him all of his life.

"Dill worked for Kruger for nearly ten years. He claims Kruger is so overextended that if he failed for one month to get the gold shipments from the mines, the banks would close him out."

Foster shook his head in bewilderment. "It doesn't make sense. Why would the banks keep on trusting him? They'd never trust me if I were overextended."

Barton's grin was wicked. "Nor me, but we aren't big operators and Kruger is. He no sooner finishes one building than he mortgages it and starts another with the mortgage money. He's building a railroad east out of Los Angeles to compete with the SP. He's bought huge ranches in Southern California and in Mexico. Dill says he lives like a prince, that his personal expenditures are more in a day than the average man spends in a year."

He broke off as Carl Dill turned from the trail and rode toward them, leading a horse.

"Any trouble?"

Dill swung down stiffly. "They're talking about the escape. Apparently the news is all over the valley. Well, we couldn't hope to hold it up long, but now I think it's more than foolish to ride into the Ferry."

"What'd you tell them about the horse?"

18 / THE NIGHT RIDERS

"That my brother and I were crossing the river, that his foundered."

"Did they believe you?"

Dill only shrugged.

Barton turned to find the men watching him. He could sense their hesitation. Clyde Miller's fear showed in his old eyes. Kid Boyd refused to meet his glance.

His tone was quiet, without emotion. "You think we're foolish, riding in?"

Emmett Foster said softly, "It's something you have to do. I'll go with you."

Surprisingly Fred Rankin spoke. "Count me in. I ain't seen a town in a long time."

Of all the men with him Barton trusted Rankin least. But he knew the man's type, steady, calm in a fight. There was a difference between a man with a gun and a gunfighter, the difference in their points of view. The man with a gun might pull it as quickly as the professional. He might even be as good a shot. But they had not the same intent.

A man with a gun, drawing that gun, might merely be trying to get the drop on his opponent. A gunfighter never raised his weapon without meaning to pull its trigger.

This intent meant a split second's difference which could well be fatal to any man.

He said, "All right. Emmett, Rankin, and I will ride in. The rest of you wait at the Crossing."

"Not me." Clyde Miller's voice might have a querulous tremor but it lacked nothing of resolution. "I go with you."

"So do I." It was Kid Boyd.

The ex-guard, Powers, nodded.

Carl Dill laughed shortly. Basically he was a mocking man, a man who took nothing in life very seriously, with the exception of his hatred of Donald Kruger.

"If you think I'm going to sweat it out here alone, think once again. Let's ride." He turned and threw Miller's saddle onto the new horse.

THE NIGHT RIDERS / 19

Mitch Barton came into Morgan's Ferry after full dark. He came alone, seeking obscurity as a solitary, casual rider.

The others followed by twos, each using a different route.

The main street was dark save for patches of lamplight thrown out from the store windows and saloon doorways. Mitch rode one block, then the second, his head bent easily forward, the soft hat pulled low.

He passed people scattered along the sidewalk. He passed half a dozen riders and two buggies. He reached the mouth of the alley beside the Oriental Saloon and swung leisurely into it.

Here he dismounted and waited in the deep shadow for the others to join him.

They came in slowly, without apparent hurry or nervousness, like tired men off the range wanting an evening's fun in town. They gathered in the alley, swinging down at Barton's side in silence.

Barton sent Kid Boyd with Rankin, west to the rear corner of the building at Nugget Street. He left Powers to hold the horses. Clyde Miller, Foster, and Dill he took with him and retraced his way to the main street corner, pausing in the alley's mouth for a long survey of the sidewalks.

Across Main Street at the darkened window of Harmon's upstairs law office Alf Kodyke cradled his Winchester and watched, his mouth a tight, thin smile, his pale blue eyes alert.

He had watched the nondescript figures disappear one by one into the alley but in the gloom he could not be certain which was Barton.

He waited, wishing now that he had brought some of his own men into town. But he had not dared. The townspeople would side with Barton. If they were alerted by seeing his mine police they might have warned Barton. Barton might not have ridden in.

Waiting was easy for Kodyke. Actually he was not too worried. His ambushes guarded all roads leading out of the Ferry. He felt secure that the escaped convicts could not pass through them.

20 / **THE NIGHT RIDERS**

Mitch Barton spoke to Dill in the alley's mouth.

"You three cover me from here. Don't come in unless you hear a racket."

His chance came then, a moment when no pedestrian was on the sidewalk between him and the saloon doorway, and he made his quick, sure-footed stride for the entrance.

The sudden movement caught Kodyke by surprise. He brought his rifle around, but too late. Already the batwing doors had flapped shut behind Barton.

Decay, old dust, and the odor of many spilled drinks assaulted Mitch Barton as he stepped to one side and paused, searching the half crowd for familiar faces. There was no one he immediately recognized and he dropped his head again so that the low-drawn hatbrim shadowed his eyes, and moved into the room toward the gambling tables at the rear.

His lined cheeks were covered by a two-day stubble of white flecked beard, grimed with dirt. He hated the dirt but at least it was a mask to lessen the prison pallor that could mark him in this collection of sun-darkened men.

And then he saw his son, very small, slight, with curling black hair, seated and almost hidden behind the faro layout.

A rush of giddiness filled Mitch Barton, and then a quick rising anger against the money-grasping woman who stood possessively at the child's side.

Looking at her face it was hard to believe that Marie Beauchamp could be anything but good and kind. She was hardly over five feet, an inch shorter than Barton's wife had been. She had the same shining black hair, the same glowing dark eyes, the small, improbable nose. She still looked like an appealing child herself although he knew that she was nearly his own age.

Her luminous gaze came up as he approached and she measured his bearded face as if some hint of his identity crossed her mind, then dropped again to the layout as her nephew dealt the next card from the *shoe*.

Barton stood there, hating her for what she was doing to the boy. The idea of a child here in this gambling hall when he should be out in the sun playing, learning to ride, to hunt, to fish, made him sick inside.

But he crowded down the feeling quickly. He could not afford the luxury of quarreling with her at the moment. Not only his life but the lives of the men who waited for him in the outer darkness depended upon his not attracting attention to himself.

He hesitated, wondering what would happen if he merely picked up the boy and dashed for the rear door. There were two dozen men within the room and most of them wore arms. The moment he touched his son the woman was bound to scream. It might be better if he grabbed her instead, pressed his gun against her side, used her soft body as a shield.

The child would certainly come with them if she told him to. They could gain the door, the horses in the alley before the men in the saloon would realize quite what had happened.

But as his intent crystallized his son dealt the last card. The woman spoke in a low, clear voice.

"The game is closed, gentlemen. It will reopen in an hour."

She nodded to the lookout perched on his high stool beyond the layout. He climbed down, slid the lid of the flat money box into place and started toward the door in the side wall below the bar.

The door to Cap Ayres' office, Barton knew. He watched, still tempted, as Marie Beauchamp took the boy's hand and led him toward the office. But he did not move, not until the door had closed behind them, until the lookout reappeared without the money box. Then he eased idly forward until he stood before the door, and turned to see if anyone in the saloon was watching.

No one seemed to be paying him any attention. He lifted the latch and slid through the opening, closing the panel softly at his back.

Three people were in the office. The third was a short man built like a block of granite, his hair a brush of gray above a

22 / THE NIGHT RIDERS

red, pouchy face. He wore a long-tailed black coat, a ruffled shirt, a string tie, striped trousers. But the hook which extended from the right coat sleeve caught the attention, for it was polished until it shown lifelike in the lamp's radiance. Its point was slender, razor-sharp. Cap Ayres.

Ayers turned, hearing the roll of sound from the gambling room as the door opened. The hook came up and out in an instinctive, threatening gesture. Then he stopped, surprise loosening the red folds of his cheeks.

"Mitch Barton." His eyes sweeping to the girl and then back. "You fool. What did you come here for?"

"For him." Barton pointed at the wide-eyed boy.

The Yankee Duchess swung with Ayres' first word, staring at Barton, full recognition coming now.

"You."

The word was a curse. Her small hands went quickly, protectively to the child's shoulders.

"You aren't going to take him."

"I am." Barton's voice was tight, uncompromising.

"He's not yours to take." It was a challenge. "You never saw him. I raised him. He's mine."

Some of the anger which had filled him when he saw the slight figure behind the faro bank rose now in his voice.

"You raised him how? In a saloon, so dollar hungry you'd sacrifice his childhood for a novelty to bring suckers to a faro bank."

"Careful, Barton." It was Ayres. "You don't know what you're talking about."

"I don't know? I just saw it. I know what Dill told me. I know this woman. She'd sell her own lifeblood for a cartwheel."

Shaking, he turned to her and saw the answering anger blaze up in her set face.

Cap Ayres reached out his hook. He passed it neatly around Mitch Barton's wrist, the needle point not touching the skin. He pulled Barton around to face him fully.

"Know something from me too, my friend. She did only what she had to do, was forced to do. Everyone has to eat, or have you forgotten that since the state has been buying your meals?"

"Her place in San Francisco fed her all right. What's she doing in the Ferry anyhow?"

"Her San Francisco place? Donald Kruger ruined that, long ago. He and his high-flying friends passed the word that her games were crooked. Before she realized what they were doing she was broke. Why did Kruger do it? For one reason only, because she's unfortunate enough to be your sister-in-law."

Barton stared at him, baffled by the intensity of the saloon man's words.

"But why did she come here, why put him at the table?"

"She went first to your ranch, which the child should inherit. She found your cousin there, and he had already sold out to Kruger's men. He told her she could stay if she married him. She laughed in his face. He ran her off. But he kept your son there, under Kruger's thumb."

Barton laughed harshly. "My son at the ranch? This is my son, here."

"She got him back."

"How?"

"I'll tell you how I got him back." It was the Duchess now, and her eyes were wet with her anger. "I got him back because Cap Ayres rode to the ranch and put the point of his hook against Finley's neck, and told him he'd push it through if we didn't get the child."

Barton gazed down at the gleaming metal which half-circled his wrist. In his own youth that hook had fascinated him, and he remembered stories of how Cap Ayres had used it in barroom fights.

Ayres for all that he was growing paunchy had once had a reputation as a fighter. No one knew for certain much about the man. He was supposed to have lost the hand at Gettysburg, but he never spoke of it.

"We brought him here and Cap gave me the faro bank. But I didn't dare leave Ralph with anyone. I kept him beside me, brought him to work, and he slept here in the office every night."

Barton stared from one to the other, suddenly oppressed by the sense that much living had gone on outside the prison walls during his years in the timeless, narrow cell.

"He won't burden you any longer," he said, and reached for the boy's hand. The Duchess whirled between them, holding the child behind her.

"No you don't."

Barton said, "You wouldn't leave him with Finley within Kruger's reach. Do you think I'll leave him where Kruger can use him as a weapon, as a hostage to keep me from fighting him?"

Marie Beauchamp gasped. "Fight Kruger? Are you crazy? You're a fugitive now. I called you a fool once. I'll call you double fool . . . for not having learned your lesson, for not seeing by now that no one fights Kruger and survives. Ride for the border, get away while you can. But this child stays with me.

"You stole my sister from me. You destroyed her voice. You killed her. I'll not let you kill her son."

Surprisingly Cap Ayres spoke, his voice suddenly tired. "Ralph can't stay here now, Marie. I can't protect him from Kruger. He's got to be taken away."

She swung on the saloon man, shocked. "Cap. Oh, Cap. I never thought you'd turn against me."

He shook his head, and the heavy face held all the sadness in the world.

"I am not turning away," he said. "There's nothing I wouldn't try to do for you. But I can't control Barton, and if Kruger wants the boy for insurance Kodyke and his mine police will ride in and take him. I'm just one man."

"What's Barton but one man?"

"He'll have the valley behind him. They'll follow him because they're desperate. I don't know what he can do. Perhaps he'll die. But the boy must be taken to a safe place. That is"—he spoke as if remembering something suddenly—"if Kodyke lets us."

The changed note in the man's voice caught Barton's ear. "If what?"

"I'm the fool." Ayres was suddenly upset, standing, snapping his fingers as if that would bring him an answer. "Seeing you, Mitch, was such a shock that I forgot. Alf Kodyke is in town. He was in the bar less than an hour ago, looking at Ralph.

"I'll lay you a bet he's figuring the boy as bait, figuring you'd do exactly what you've done, come here. I think you're in a trap, Barton. It'll be your life or your son's."

CHAPTER FOUR

MITCH BARTON was alert, impatient. "Who is Kodyke?"

"A killer." Ayres groaned. "As truly a gunman as I've ever seen, and I've seen quite a few. Head of Kruger's mine police. I don't know what he's done before, but I know what he's done in the valley.

"After you went to prison a few of the ranchers tried to continue the fight. They stopped two gold shipments, turned them back. They cut another flume. Then Kodyke appeared. Some of the Night Riders just vanished. Others were given twelve hours to leave the country. One didn't. He was beaten to death."

"That doesn't sound like much security for the boy even if I let them take me. Does it, Duchess?" Barton said.

He looked at the girl, seeing that the color had drained from her, seeing her shake her head slowly and shudder.

"None. Not even if you were dead."

26 / THE NIGHT RIDERS

He began to pace the office as he had so often paced his prison cell, thinking desperately.

"Cap, is there anyone in town we could trust for help? Anyone who would stand up against this man?"

Cap Ayres lifted his shoulders and let them drop. "He's probably got his whole damn' gang with him. He's just as popular as the plague and the town fears him more. You can't blame them. Even to help the child. There'd be reprisals, and they have children of their own."

Barton stopped abruptly before Ayres, a twisting look almost of mirth breaking on his stiff face.

"The plague? That's it, Cap. The plague. Is Doc Wilson still around?"

The saloon man nodded, his eyes narrowing, watching Barton.

"Send someone for him. Don't let anyone come in here. Have a wagon brought down from the livery, then go out the rear door and over to the alley. I've got six men there, some you know. Tell them to pull out singly and meet me at Dutch Flat, but not to leave until the wagon does. Bring Rankin here, but be careful."

Still Ayres stood, searching for alternatives. Finally he sighed.

"You've played hell, haven't you? Marie, we've got to try it. It's the only chance to get Ralph to safety."

"Go." It was the Duchess. "Do it."

Ayres moved then, disappearing through the door. Barton turned quickly and squatted before the boy, bringing his face down almost on a level with the child's.

"Ralph, do you know who I am?"

The dark eyes bordered by their fringe of long, curling lashes met his uncertainly.

"I guess you're my father."

Barton wanted suddenly to touch him, to hold him close.

"I am. What do you know about me?"

Color flushed the smooth olive cheeks. "Well, not much. I know you are . . . I mean you *were* in prison."

"Do you know why?"

The child shook his head. "Because you did something bad, I guess."

Barton's eyes went up to the watching woman. "What did you tell him?"

Her face also had gained a flush. "Nothing. But others have. You don't think it was a secret?"

"Did you tell him I was against violence, that I was trying to follow the law?"

"You were their leader." Her deep feeling made her voice sound coarse.

He let it pass. There was no time for argument now.

He spoke again to the boy, slowly and earnestly. "You're pretty young, but by the way you've been raised you probably understand more than most boys your age would. There is a man, maybe more than one, in this town who wants to kill us. It depends on you whether or not we can get away from him. Do you think you can pretend to be sick, very sick, enough to make people believe you?"

The eyes which had watched him almost fearfully lit with a growing curiosity.

"What kind of sick?"

"Like with smallpox. Do you know what that is?"

The small figure took a backward step. "Old Bell had it last year. They put him in his cabin and shoved food under the door. He died."

"You aren't going to die," Barton said. "But you must pretend to be very sick."

The girl reached for the child's shoulder. "It will never work."

Barton rose, towering above her. "Have you a better idea?"

She did not answer.

"Do you know this Kodyke?"

"I've seen him."

"Do you think he'd kill you, kill the boy if it served his purpose?"

She drew a slow breath. "He would. He reminds me of a snake."

"Then we have to try. I know you hate me. I know you blame me..."

She made a small sweeping gesture with her hand. "That doesn't matter now."

"No," he said. "What does matter is Ralph. Whether we get him clear may depend on you both." He stretched his hand toward the child and behind him heard Cap Ayres come back into the office and turned swiftly.

"I talked to your boys," the saloon man said. "Rankin says he's not known here. He's out at the bar."

"Bring him in."

Rankin came through the door. His green eyes flickered at sight of the Duchess, then turned questioningly on Barton.

Quickly Mitch told him of the probable ambush, and the gunman grinned.

"When Doc Wilson comes," Barton went on, "he's going to tell the crowd out there that the child has smallpox. If I know people they'll scatter like quail, and the news will be all over town in five minutes. This Kodyke, if he's around, will hear it.

"If Doc and the Duchess load Ralph in the wagon and head out for the doctor's ranch the chances are that Kodyke won't try to stop them. If he does, I'll be in the wagon.

"Wait until we're clear of town, then you and the boys ride out one at a time. If Kodyke's people are watching the north road now they won't be by the time you get there."

Rankin nodded. Whatever his faults, he caught on rapidly. As he turned toward the door he gave the Duchess a second slow, measuring look.

Barton saw it. He glanced quickly at Marie Beauchamp, but her eyes were on the splintered boards of the floor. No one spoke. The door closed behind Rankin. The silence in the room grew oppressive before Barton broke it to say, "Has Ralph any warm clothes here?"

The girl shook her head. "I could go down to the house. It's only a few doors along Nugget . . ."

"No chance. Kodyke's men may be watching the place."

"He'll need a coat. And I'll have to have something other than this to ride in." She fingered the lace, the draped folds of the red taffeta dress.

"Borrow Cap's coat," said Barton. "You're only going as far as Doc Wilson's."

The Duchess seemed to grow taller. She lifted her head defiantly. "I'm going with Ralph."

Barton shook his head.

"No. A woman in a gang of men means trouble whoever she is. And you could destroy our whole plan. Also we'll be living in an abandoned mine. The buildings are twenty years old and they weren't much to start with."

"The more reason he will need me." It was a flat statement, final.

Before he could argue further a roll of knuckles rattled on the door. Barton put his hand on his gun, and Cap Ayres called, "Who is it?"

"Wilson."

"Come on in, Doc."

The door opened on a small gray-haired man. Despite his age Hal Wilson moved on his bandy legs with a quick decisiveness which would have done credit to a far younger man.

He came in saying, "What's the matter with the boy? Joe Kamps said he was pretty sick. I . . ." He stopped. He stared at Mitch Barton, his blue eyes narrowing.

"Mitch. You damn' fool. What are you doing in the Ferry? This is the last place you should have come, man. The very last place."

Mitch let go of the gun. "Hi, Doc." He had known Wilson a very long time. The small doctor had brought him into the world.

"You've got to get out of here." Wilson, who liked to pose as the quietest of men, was in reality one of the most excitable. "I saw Kodyke in town little more than an hour ago. The place will be swarming with mine police."

Barton nodded. "That's why we sent for you. Ralph has the smallpox."

The doctor spun to the boy. "He's got *what?* Why, you're crazy, man. He's no more sick than . . ."

"I say he has smallpox. And you're going to say he has smallpox. You're going to say it very loudly, in the bar."

The doctor's eyes crinkled at the corners. "You know what would happen?"

"I know what will happen. Every man jack out there will run like a rabbit. The news will be all over town in a matter of minutes. You will have the boy carried out, loaded into a wagon and with the Duchess you will drive him to your ranch for quarantine."

"And if Kodyke stops us?"

"I'll be in the wagon, under a blanket."

The doctor pursed his lips. "I suppose you realize that you're risking the child's life? That you're risking Miss Beauchamp's?"

Barton said, "Doc, one thing prison taught me. To face realities. I have no choice. Kodyke wants my son as hostage for me. How safe would he be with Kodyke?"

Wilson hesitated a moment longer, then he headed for the doorway. Barton moved across to Cap Ayres' peephole. Through it he could see the whole rear section of the room. He saw Wilson stop, put his back to the bar so that he faced the room and wiped his forehead with his large handkerchief. He heard the doctor raise his voice.

"Now there's nothing to get excited about. . . . I want you all to remain calm."

His words cut through the waves of noise and it eddied to a stop. Every head turned to look at him, even the players at the poker tables lifted their eyes.

Wilson spread his hands. "I'm sure all of you will be sorry to hear it, but the Tiger has got the smallpox."

A stunned silence swallowed the room, then broke in a babble of voices. Already men swayed, edging toward the front door. In less than three minutes the big saloon was empty.

CHAPTER FIVE

ALF KODYKE WATCHED from his place at the window as the crowd spilled from the Oriental Saloon. He heard the loud arguments below. He made out the dread word, *pox,* and knew how fearful the valley was of the disease. Only three years before it had killed thirty people in the ranch houses scattered through the lower hills.

Without hesitation he rose and, carrying his rifle loosely in the crook of his arm, went down the broken stairs to the street. The first man he buttonholed told indignantly what had happened.

By nature Kodyke was a suspicious man. The idea of the boy becoming suddenly sick just as Barton appeared in town was too much for him to swallow.

His impulse was to cross and go into the saloon. He had no doubt of his own ability to face Barton, to drop the escaped convict in an exchange of gunplay. But he was also conscious of the other six riders who had drifted into the shelter of the alley, and he had no intention of subjecting himself to their cross fire.

He stood where he was, inconspicuous, for the sidewalk around him was crowded now with watching people, people careful to keep the width of the road between themselves and the wagon that rattled up from the livery.

The doctor came out of the saloon. Cap Ayres followed, carrying the blanketed boy. Marie Beauchamp trailed them with other blankets from the couch in Ayres' office. These she arranged in the bed of the wagon, and the boy was laid on them gently. Then she and the doctor climbed to the wagon seat and it moved off slowly down the unlit road.

The darkness hid Mitch Barton, waiting around the corner of the distant intersecting cross street. As the wagon passed he slipped forward, over the tailgate, and crawled beneath the blankets next to his son.

The boy's small body was trembling and Mitch whispered softly, "Easy, Ralph, there's nothing to worry about."

"I'm not worrying." The childish voice had a choked sound which belied his words.

The wagon rumbled on. Kodyke watched its blurred shape, waiting for Barton's men to appear from the alley mouth.

They did not appear. There was no sign of Barton. The fugitive could have slid out of the saloon's rear door, of course, but still Kodyke was not disturbed. The men would not be allowed to pass the roadblock beyond the bridge.

He left the excited crowd, finding his horse, mounting and riding casually down Main Street toward the northern bridge. He gave no appearance of hurry. The wagon moved along a thousand yards ahead of him, its team plodding, indifferent to the doctor's urging.

Kodyke chuckled. The smallpox scare might spook the citizens of the Ferry but it had no terrors for him. He had had the pox in Kansas ten years before.

The wagon wheels made hollow sounds upon the loose timbers of the bridge and then started up the steep bank beyond the river. At the top the team halted, and Kodyke saw his four riders come out to circle it, saw them etched against the background of the lighter sky.

He put spurs to his horse. In a minute he would find out just how sick the boy was. Circumstances seemed to have played directly into his hands.

He did not even need to face the anger of an aroused town to take the child out of the Ferry. They had conveniently taken him out themselves. He rode across the bridge and up the rise.

Wilson was standing in the wagon, gesticulating, his voice loud with authority.

"Stay back, I tell you. The boy has the pox, you fool. Do you want the pox? I'm taking him out of town before the infection spreads."

Kodyke saw that his men kept a respectful distance. He grinned, a cold, calculating grin.

"A wise precaution, Doctor. But it doesn't apply to me. You see, sir, I have been unfortunate, or shall I say fortunate enough to have suffered and survived the plague. I'll just look at the patient and decide for myself how bad it is."

He spoke to the doctor but his eyes were on the woman, and he wished he could see her face more clearly in the starlight. She bothered him as few women ever had.

She said now in a suppressed voice, "Are you trying to kill the child? What kind of man are you?"

He rode closer, until his stirrup scraped against the wagon's front wheel. His face was nearly level with hers as she sat on the high seat.

"Duchess," he said, "I know you've heard hard stories about me, but remember that they have been told by my enemies. I have nothing against the boy, but I am going to find Mitchell Barton and send him back to prison where he belongs."

He stopped for a full minute to give his words effect. "From what I hear you have good cause to hate him. You should be willing to co-operate. If you do, I give you my word that nothing will harm the child."

For a moment she hesitated. Then she shook her head.

"That can wait. Take my word that the boy is ill. Don't uncover him here. A chill would be fatal, with the pox."

Beneath the dark blanket Barton tensed. One arm rested on his son's shoulder and he felt the trembling. His other hand gripped his unholstered gun. If Kodyke reached into the wagon

34 / THE NIGHT RIDERS

box and lifted the blanket he would find the cold muzzle within inches of his face.

But Kodyke did not move the blanket for the Duchess went on.

"If you insist on examining Ralph, ride to the doctor's house. He must not be exposed to the night air any more than necessary."

She had no real plan behind the words. She wanted foremost to avoid a showdown on the dark road, a discovery that might endanger the child. And luck was with her. The Duchess had the confirmed gambler's belief in luck. She had seen it proved many times. Anyone, even a professional with the house odds behind him, needed a fair share of luck to sit in any game. And Marie Beauchamp believed in her luck.

Kodyke relaxed. This he liked. It meant a chance to see her again, by lamplight, a chance to talk to her. He had the vanity of his kind and knew that he stirred curiosity at least in most women.

He said to the doctor, "All right. Drive on," and held his horse as the wagon creaked into slow motion. Then he turned back toward his men, noting with amusement that they kept a safe distance from him.

These men were as tough a crew as he had been able to find. He had recruited them carefully, and he had been extremely blunt.

"I don't care what your crimes were before you came to work for the company, but if you ever cross me I'll personally kill you."

They had obeyed him, and he fully expected obedience now.

He said, "I'm going to ride on with the doctor. There won't be any trouble there that I can't handle. You stay here. Barton will probably be along. He's got six men with him, but if you catch them on the bridge that should finish it."

He wheeled his horse without expecting a reply and cantered after the slow-paced wagon. He rode at Marie Beauchamp's side, and she talked to him, questioning him about his own bout with the pox, keeping his attention with practiced ease.

Doc Wilson's ranch was two miles from the Ferry. The house topped a small knoll above the river, high enough that the yard itself had remained untouched by the recurring floods.

Wilson turned at last through the gate and drove up beside the porch, climbing down heavily. He swung and helped the girl to the ground and she moved toward the rear of the wagon. But Kodyke was before her, dropping the tailgate, reaching in, pulling off the blankets.

Barton sat up as the cover left his shoulders, and Kodyke stared into the barrel of the revolver.

There was a moment of full stillness, then Barton made a little jerking motion with his gun which was more expressive than any words.

Kodyke slowly raised his hands.

"Turn around."

The gunman turned deliberately. Barton jumped from the wagon bed, his gun held ready. He put it against the middle of Kodyke's back and reached around to lift the revolver from the other's belt.

Kodyke moved faster than Barton had dreamed was possible. His right hand dropped to close on Barton's wrist and his lithe body twisted snakelike in a pivoting turn. Barton's gun exploded. The bullet cut across the shoulders of Kodyke's coat without penetrating the skin.

Then Barton was jerked from his feet as Kodyke threw himself backward.

The gun slipped from Barton's fingers as they fell. Kodyke had released his grip on Barton's wrist and was trying desperately to roll away, to draw his own gun at the same time.

Barton went after him, scrambling on hands and knees. He reached him just as the heavy gun came free, and seized its barrel before Kodyke could raise it from the ground.

For a moment they were motionless, Kodyke straining to bring up the weapon, Barton fighting to prevent him.

THE NIGHT RIDERS

Then suddenly Kodyke let go and drove his fist hard into Barton's face, jarring him backward. But if he had hoped that Barton would relinquish his hold on the barrel he was disappointed.

Barton clung to it even as he went over onto his back. Kodyke was upon him with the quickness of a panther, striking with both hands, hammering at Mitch's face.

Barton tried to reverse the gun and lost it under the rain of jabbing blows. He rolled to escape the punishing fists, came up to his knees and then to his feet.

Kodyke came up with him and they stood, their bodies pressed together, pounding each other's ribs, and the gunman was the first to give ground. He backed off. Barton let him go, wiping the heel of his hand across his face.

It came away red from the broken nose and he shook his head to clear his vision, then jumped in, for Kodyke had reached down, had drawn a vicious bladed knife from his boot top.

He slashed out at Barton's rush, but Barton side-stepped, grabbing the knife wrist with both hands. Twisting, Barton threw the point of his hip into Kodyke's side and levered the arm down until the wrist threatened to snap.

Slowly the man's fingers relaxed, the knife fell to the ground. Still Barton continued the pressure, until the man went to his knees. Then Barton stepped away, released the wrist and kneed Kodyke under the chin. The man went over on his shoulder, tried to get up and Barton hit him hard in the back of the neck, twice, and saw him drop forward onto his face and lie unmoving in the dust of the yard.

He dived onto the prone figure, then rolled free as he felt its limpness. Slowly he got to his feet, cautious with disbelief.

He was so near exhaustion that he staggered as he stepped over to retrieve the fallen guns, the knife. He knew that if Kodyke had lasted but a few minutes longer the fight would have gone the other way.

His years of inactivity at the prison had taken their toll. He simply did not have the stamina which once had been his.

The boy still huddled in the wagon bed, his eyes very large. Marie Beauchamp ran to him and the doctor closed in on Barton.

"Let me look at that nose."

"It's all right. Where can I lock him up?"

"The woodshed. There's a bar across the door."

Barton stooped, gathering up the unconscious Kodyke and half-carried, half-dragged him to the small building. He dumped him inside unceremoniously, dropped the bar in place and limped back toward the wagon.

Wilson said sharply, "You'd better take these two and keep going."

"Get them dressed to travel. I'll be back."

He had reached Kodyke's horse when the distant shot jarred the night, and he flung himself up, wheeled the animal around and drove out of the yard.

The firing ahead became a steady barrage. Barton pulled the horse in a little, easing the gait to a strong run which ate up the distance.

He saw the flash of gunfire long before he saw the bridge, and by it spotted the positions of Kodyke's men. They crouched behind a stone wall surrounding Wilson's old orchard. Other flashes located his own crew, scattered on the far side of the river, unable to cross.

It was a stalemate. Apparently the mine police were content to pin the others down, to await Kodyke's return.

Barton pulled Kodyke's Winchester from its boot, checking it by touch, and swung off the road short of the broken wall. He paralleled its dark shape, sifting among the trees. The trunks were all dead, long since killed by the smothering silt built up by the recurring floods. He came quietly, the gun ready, behind the mine police, until he reached a corner post still standing. From there he laid one shot after another against the wall.

38 / THE NIGHT RIDERS

He cared not whether he hit anyone. These were only hired guns, and he had no desire to kill except where killing was necessary.

Caught by surprise by the firing behind them, Kodyke's men swung and sought through the darkness with their bullets, but could not find him. They stood only a minute, then broke for their horses.

He heard the thunder of their passage as they drove east, cutting directly across the country. When they were well gone he raised his voice and heard Carl Dill answer, and rode down to the bridge.

Not until he reached the abutment did he see the sprawled figure on the splintered planks.

He stepped from the horse, going quickly to bend over the fallen man, to recognize Clyde Miller. Gently he touched the quiet shoulder, and bitterness rose in him anew. He was still there when the others walked forward through the gloom.

Dill's voice spoke tightly. "We came out one at a time, as you said. Clyde was first. They shot him out of the saddle without even a challenge. He might have been just anyone."

Barton wished now that he had aimed more carefully at the men behind the wall. He would not make that mistake again.

They brought up the horses, lifted Miller's body across his saddle and turned up the bank to the doctor's ranch. On the way Barton told them of his fight with Kodyke, and as they reached the yard Dill laughed harshly.

"So we've got him, let's hang him. He's their boss, and more responsible than anyone for Clyde's death. It will be a warning to the rest."

Instinctively Barton shook his head. "No. None of that."

"What's the matter?" It was Fred Rankin. "If you're going to fight you'd better fight to win."

Barton looked at the grim, tight faces, seeing that their minds were set. There was no way he could halt the hanging short of violence, and Kodyke alive would always be a danger to them.

"Get him," he said.

He swung down, eased Miller from the horse and carried the old man to the porch. A sudden yell from the woodhouse brought him around. Dill and Rankin had found a lantern, had lighted it and opened the barred door.

"He's gone."

Barton ran across the yard. The woodshed was empty. Kodyke had managed to loosen two boards in the rear wall. He had made his escape.

They tried to trail him, but in the darkness, in the dry grass they could find no track. Slowly they turned back, silent with uneasiness.

They buried Miller with no time for ceremony, then went in to the doctor and prepared to ride again.

CHAPTER SIX

Alf Kodyke had regained consciousness in time to hear the racket of the battle at the bridge through the thin walls of the old woodshed. It was completely dark in the small confine and he woke with a sense of floating, of turning over and over slowly in the void of blackness.

He shook his head, feeling beneath it the roughness of wood chips, and then with his hands explored the ground around him. His right hand touched chill metal, his fingers identified an ax blade, and he relaxed. He knew where he was.

Getting to his feet was painful. Mitchell Barton may have been long in prison but he could still hit hard. He would be an adversary worth fighting. Kodyke almost laughed to himself. The boy and Marie Beauchamp would be in the doctor's house, and probably Barton would be with them. All he needed to do was break out of this shed and get to his men at the river. They would be finished with the ambush of the Night Riders and could close in to complete their job here.

It took him awhile to search the shed, feeling along the walls with his hands, inching his feet around the chunks of unseen wood. Then he felt moving air on his face and sought its source, discovering a wide crack between two of the upright boards where a batten had fallen away. Into this he slid the ax blade and, using the handle as a lever, pried the board free from its holding nails. They clung for a moment in the dry grip of the wood, and then the board sprang out at the bottom, hanging loosely by the top fastening. He pried free the board next to it and a moment later crawled through the gap into the fresh night air.

He stood a minute listening, and heard the running noises of approaching horses and made a quick dash for the corner of the doctor's house, expecting his men but being cautious by long habit.

The horses came close. He recognized the light jingle of silver on Cornish's Mexican saddle and stepped away from the building. But the horses ran on, passed the doctor's turn and their sound faded down the road heading for the mine.

Kodyke cursed silently, knowing now that the fight had gone the other way. He looked across the yard toward the wagon, seeing the two horses standing, still hitched, and seeing that his own horse was gone. His hand tightened on the ax and he started for the wagon. He would have to ride without a saddle, but that would be almost a pleasure beside the disciplining he would contrive for his men.

And then he had another thought. Barton's crew would surely come here again, for the boy. Kodyke was unarmed except for the ax, but if he could stay out of sight, if he could listen, he might learn where they were headed next. He smiled thinly.

There was little hiding place in the grassed and rockstrewn area within listening distance. And probably Barton would

THE NIGHT RIDERS / 41

search for him when they found him missing from the woodshed. But there was one good place for him.

Light glowed from the front of the house and from one window that should open to a bedroom, but the kitchen wing was dark, single storied and low roofed, and there was a porch supported by thin posts. Kodyke walked toward it sliding the ax handle beneath his belt at his back.

With the care of a stalking cat he climbed, inching up the near post until his fingers grappled over the edge of the roof, pulling upward and spreading both hands flat on the rough shakes and then like a caterpillar working higher. Balanced delicately because of the roof's overhang he unwrapped his legs from the post and eased one up and caught the toe of his boot on the upper side of the sloping surface. From there it was easier.

When Barton led his riders into the doctor's yard Alf Kodyke lay flat in the darker angle where the pitch of the main roof came down to join the flatter porch. He lay unmoving, and listened.

He heard them arrive and heard Barton approve the verdict to hang him. He listened to the scrabbling noises of the search and followed part of it by the zigzag path of the man who carried the lantern. Then he heard their return and their hollow steps as they mounted the front porch and went into the house. He moved then for the first time, turning to place his ear close against the roof.

Apparently no one went into the kitchen. Kodyke could hear the low mumble of voices without being able to distinguish a word. But still he waited. He could not go down, unarmed against the several desperate men.

He wished that he had used his time to enter the house. He could have handled the doctor and woman, could have gone with the boy before Barton came back, but he had expected Barton to be in the house also.

He moved again, creeping silently up the angle of the main roof to its ridge and stretching out along its back slope. There was little chance of his being spotted, for the night was moonless and the lantern's rays would not lift so far.

Kodyke was a patient man and the patience was rewarded when at last the front door reopened, spilling more light onto the yard, and the men came again from the house.

He heard the boy's sleepy, tremulous voice.

"Where are we going now?"

He heard the girl's soft tone answer but again could make out no word. He heard the confusion of their mounting and then they were gone. There had not been a word spoken in the yard of any help to him.

He waited until the sounds died out along the road before he slid down the roof and dropped to the ground, hurrying to the house corner for a swift survey of the yard. The wagon was still there, one horse still in harness. And Kodyke smiled.

Soundlessly he stepped to the porch and put his face against the curtained glass of the door. Through it he could see a shadow move. He put his left hand on the knob and with his right drew the ax from his belt. Then he opened the door and stepped inside in one quick movement.

Doc Wilson turned without haste, only the flicker of his eyes showing his surprise at seeing Kodyke, seeing the thin smile on the snakelike face.

"Doctor," Kodyke said, "your patient recovered quickly. I want to know where they have taken him."

Doc Wilson shrugged, his expression not changing. "I have no idea. I insisted that they not tell me. Take the wagon back to town, you can get a horse there."

Kodyke took a single step forward, lifting the ax and twisting it so that the lamplight flashed from its edges.

"I don't believe you, Doctor, and I have no time to play questions and answers. Where did Barton go?"

Wilson stood where he was beside the cloth-covered center table, the outspread fingers of his right hand pressed tensely on the top of a book. He shook his head.

"You can save your time. I don't know where they went."

Kodyke moved like a striking rattler. In two steps he was on the doctor, standing behind him with his left arm thrown around the other man and pinning the right hand where it lay. He moved the ax over the hand, brushing it enough to draw the loosening old skin into ridges.

"Once more, Doctor, and every time I have to ask after this it will cost you a finger."

Wilson was no longer young and he was excitable until it came to the matter of doctoring. Then the habit of years settled him, his judgment was clear and true and his knife, if he had to operate, was as steady as in his youth. He looked down at his hand now, the hand that had held the knife so many times.

He did not struggle. He stood perfectly still, his face showing nothing of the rage that swelled in him.

"Kodyke," he said, "if you maim me you'll help Barton more than by anything else you could do. I am the only doctor in this area. I have saved the lives of your own men. The people here will hunt you down. I thought you could think straighter than this."

Kodyke brought the ax down swiftly, barely beyond the ends of the doctor's fingers, chopping deep into the book.

"Where is Barton?"

Wilson closed his eyes. "You can cut off the whole arm and I still couldn't tell you. But they might have gone to the Ione pit, knowing you aren't there to stop a raid."

He felt the man against him stiffen. And then Kodyke released him, stepping back and around the table and studying the doctor's face for a long moment. Finally he nodded.

"That might be. But if I find you're lying, old man, I'll come back."

Still Wilson stood unmoving but he was unable to keep the contempt completely from his eyes. He watched Kodyke back to the door and through it, heard him run across the porch and slash free the harness that tied the horse to the wagon. He

44 / **THE NIGHT RIDERS**

heard the animal pound out of his yard. And then the doctor fainted.

Kodyke was in a hurry now. Wilson's suggestion that Barton had gone to the Ione pit might be a lie, but it could not be risked. Most of the mine police had been drawn off and were still staked out along the several roads from Morgan's Ferry. Creighton Hague would have only six men to defend the hydraulic operation, for Kodyke himself had established the rule that the miners could not carry arms.

He drove the horse as fast as he could and stay on its bare back. Still it was dawn before he reached Ione. The canyon leading up to the face now being worked was steep, narrow, and heavily wooded, but he rode steadily. He knew every foot of the area and in his mind he saw each of the spots where an ambush might be made for him. Short of the first of these places he turned the animal from the road into the timber and rode cautiously to the crest of the rising ridge. The smell of the pines was strong, freshening him, lifting from him some of the tiredness of the sleepless, active night.

He walked the last half mile. The crystal morning air acted like a magnifying glass in the mountains, and on horseback he could make a prime target for some hidden drygulcher.

But he saw no one nor was there any attack and long before he came into the clearing at the bottom of the mountain he heard the steady howl of the giant monitors. They had not been stopped.

He halted on the height where the ridge he was following flanked the bowl of the canyon opposite the open face, making a careful survey of the operation it was his job to protect.

On the uphill side of that face hung the wooden chutes which led the cascading water down from the great reservoir two miles higher in the hills. The chutes had not been tampered with. Their water dropped down the long almost vertical grade and into the huge canvas and leather hoses that lay on the ground like fat snakes studded with heavy rivets. The other end of the hoses were headed with long brass nozzles, tapered

THE NIGHT RIDERS / 45

to a six-inch mouth where the falling water built to a terrific pressure as the nozzles choked down its jet.

No number of men could hold those hoses. The nozzles were mounted on tripods, pivoted to be aimed toward the foot of the mountain ahead of them, and the stream fired from them ate relentlessly against the cemented sand.

There were twenty hoses at Ione, each blasting at its restricted arc, undermining the whole mountain. At intervals a slot would be driven deep enough that the cliff above no longer had support. Then a section of the face would begin to move, would drop, thundering an avalanche of sand and rock, of flailing trees onto the canyon's floor, and the nozzles would attack the slide.

Kodyke sat and watched in fascination. It always gave him a sense of exultation to follow the power, to see the conquest of the ancient hill, to realize the might of water. Against the fence of upright railroad rails the trees were caught, and then the grislies held back the rocks too big and too hard for the sluices. But most of the mountain went into the heavy wooden ditches, washed down the grade, tumbled by the iron rail riffles until it dropped its gold behind it. Then the solids that had been the mountain went on down the river channels, out of the way to make room for more.

Kodyke could see no interruption in the normal pattern of the mine and turned again upgrade toward the headquarters. Before he came out of the timber he stopped again, studying the entire area. There was no sign of the Night Riders, or that they had been here. Satisfied at last he mounted and rode into the clearing and straight to the low log office.

Huff came out of the police building, staring at Kodyke and at the saddleless horse, but did not voice his curiosity. Kodyke slid tiredly down and threw the lines toward his man.

"Have any of the crew come in yet?"

Huff nodded. "They're all in. When Barton's gang got through the bridge Joe circled back and rounded up the rest."

He knew they had been beaten but he did not risk a smile.

46 / THE NIGHT RIDERS

Kodyke would be in no mood for jokes. He took the horse and headed for the corral. Kodyke watched after him with vacant eyes, breathing deeply, ordering his thoughts and the manner in which he would tell Hague of the night's blunders.

It would be an unpleasant interview. Above all things, Kodyke resented having to admit failure. Further, he was fully aware of Hague's ill-hidden jealousy, for Kodyke worked directly under Kruger.

The chill of the morning reached him now that he was no longer exercising, making him conscious of the salty sweat dried on his skin. He was instinctively clean. He would have liked to wash before reporting but intuition told him that delay would increase his disadvantage. Hague would already know from the returned police that Barton had won the first engagement.

He rolled a brown cigarette and walked into the headquarters. Hague was at his desk, watching the door like a hungry dog. Kodyke did not wait for Hague's question.

"Barton has his son and the Duchess and five men with him. They left Morgan's Ferry about midnight, probably headed out of the country."

Hague got up from his desk and moved about nervously, shifting to the windows, then coming back to say heavily, "You don't know Barton, and you don't know this valley, and you don't know the people in it.

"Without leadership they are nothing, but Barton, the news that he is free will stir them as nothing else could. If we don't stop him, find him, he'll have two hundred men riding at his back within a week."

Kodyke resented the criticism in the other's voice. "We'll find him."

"How? You had your chance last night and let it get away. Believe me it might not come again. They can scatter through the hills and you can't come within a mile of them. Every hill rancher will be a spy for them, a source of food, a place to get fresh horses."

Kodyke said shortly, "I know that."

"And we have nearly three hundred miles of open ditches, of flumes, of dams and water basins to protect."

"I know all that too."

"Then do something about it." There was dismissal in Hague's tone, but there was also fear. It told Kodyke something about the man, something he stowed in his hard mind for future reference. Hague could not stand uncertainty, the mounting pressure, the knowledge that a revolt was building in the country around him. When the open fight came, if it did, he could not depend on Creighton Hague.

CHAPTER SEVEN

SO BEGAN THE MANHUNT. Every sheriff, every deputy in the four foothill counties joined the pack and Kodyke used his mine police as if they were an army, setting them to comb the hills for sign of Barton and his men.

Their very action played in Barton's favor for most of the small ranchers were hesitating, their sympathies with the men holed up at the old Haskell mine yet fearful that by joining them they would lose what little they had left.

The reign of terror unleashed by Kodyke in his effort to track down his quarry frightened some, but others who might have remained at home, quietly caught up their horses and vanished into the timber.

Joe Moss for one. A quiet, taciturn man unloved by any of his neighbors, he was replacing a broken pole in his corral on the fourth morning after Barton's escape. He heard the horses in the lane twisting back through the draw to his ranch yard. He straightened as they rode in, five men with Kodyke himself at their head. He leaned against the ax he had been using to trim the pole.

48 / THE NIGHT RIDERS

Kodyke almost rode him down, putting his horse so close that Moss flinched away, sitting his saddle with the easy grace of mastery which characterized his every move.

"Where's Barton?"

Moss stared up into the reptile eyes and read death there and was afraid. He was not a valiant man, a fact he had long recognized within himself. It was this knowledge of his own shortcomings that had soured him against the world. It had made him withdraw as an armadillo into its shell to protect himself from the fancied slights which galled him constantly.

"I don't know."

Kodyke, for him, was being pleasant. "There's ten thousand dollars to any man who turns him in."

Moss considered. Never in his hardscrabble life had he had ten thousand dollars or ever dreamed of having half that amount, but there seemed to him a note of mocking contempt in Kodyke's voice. It turned him surly.

"Who wants blood money?"

Kodyke struck him then. The motion was so rapid that Moss had no chance to step away. The gloved hand swept down, lifting the heavy gun from the holster at his hip, swinging it in a small arc to crack against Moss's head just above the ear.

Had the blow caught the temple it probably would have killed. But it was cushioned by the thick cap of hair, uncut for months and matted with grease and dirt.

Moss went down but he did not black out. He lay curled on his side for a full minute, his head buzzing with the low-keyed drone of angry bees. Then he came up, slowly, his hand still grasping the haft of the ax.

He had no plan. Had he even thought he would have quailed away from the suicidal idea of attempting retaliation against these men.

He swung the ax in pure, bitter reflex. The blade caught the foreleg of Kodyke's horse, chopping through to the bone. The frightened animal went up onto its hind legs, screaming as it rose and Kodyke, caught utterly by surprise, was pitched out of the saddle backward.

That he lit on his feet was due to his instinctive catlike quality. He might have shot Moss easily. Instead he leaped in, shocked to the need for physical contact. His gun lashed up and down in quick, brutal blows, cutting the man's face to ribbons, driving him to the ground to writhe sobbing in the dust.

Even when Moss lay motionless Kodyke continued to strike, and not one of those who followed him dared to interfere. Finally, satiated, he dropped the bloody gun back into its place, turned and walked to where his men had caught the injured horse.

The animal stood trembling, blood leaking from the gash on its leg. Strangely Kodyke was always kind with horses. It was one of the perversities about him that where he shed no mercy on humans he had never mistreated any animal.

He examined the cut silently, then used the handkerchief from his own neck to bind it as tightly as he could. Afterward he removed the saddle and bridle. Fashioning a hackamore from a rope he ordered the animal led to the veterinary in the nearest town.

That done he caught up Moss's horse from the corral, tied it to a post and threw his saddle on it.

His motions were as studied as if he had planned them for weeks. He turned, climbed the porch step and entered the log house. A fire smoldered in the battered cook stove perched on two wobbly legs and two stones. He kicked the stones loose, kicked the stove over so that its lids rolled away and the hot coals showered out on the splintered floor. He found a half-filled lamp and smashed it in the coals, watching the oil fluff into a white cloud.

There was a delayed flash, a dull concussion, a lightning sheet of flame.

Kodyke threw papers and clothes onto the blaze, then

50 / THE NIGHT RIDERS

walked deliberately back into the yard followed by a lazily rising plume of smoke.

Moss had managed to sit up, his battered face buried in his hands, blood and dirt drying in the cracks between his fingers. Kodyke stood over him, considering. His men shifted their horses wordlessly until they formed a rough circle. Kodyke's voice was harsh.

"Where is he?"

Moss looked up. His cut lips moved, his words were mushy. "I don't know."

Kodyke let silence run on, debating with himself whether it was worth while to further maul the man before him.

The flames now ate at the sod roof of the house, billowing orange and black from the windows and the doors. Moss watched them with glazed eyes as if not realizing that they were devouring everything he owned.

Kodyke dug a toe ungently into his ribs. "That's for trying to help Barton. You can pass the word, man. I'll have him if I have to burn every house in the valley." He swung away then, untied Moss's horse, lifted himself into the saddle and wheeled out of the yard.

Moss sat where he was, not having the strength to move, to care. The house burned on, the dry wood crackling in protest at being consumed. He watched the roof fall in, cascading sparks into the sky, and at last came uncertainly to his feet. Wobbling as if from too much alcohol he moved down to the edge of the bubbling creek. He knelt, leaning forward to bathe his bloody face, then lost his balance and plunged headlong into the foot deep water.

He managed somehow to pull himself out but he was trembling when he squatted back on his haunches, knowing that but for his last atom of strength he would have drowned.

He lay back on the soft grass of the bank, his bloodied shirt wet and clinging to his tortured body. He slept.

The sun was well down, barely above the rim of trees when he stirred. For long minutes he lay in a half stupor, too beat to care, to realize exactly what had happened to him. Then he sat up, slowly, at last seeing the pile of ashes, the still smoldering beams which had been his home.

A dull rage began, deepening until he forgot the hurt of his beaten face. He got to his feet unsteadily. He walked to the corral fence and leaned against it. The pack mule, his only other animal, came along the fence inquiringly, perhaps lonesome without the horse, perhaps brought forward by a growing thirst.

He stared at it, his sight half-obscured by swollen lids, then he got his scarred saddle from its place on the fence, wrestled it doggedly onto the animal's knifelike back and dragged himself up.

It was well after midnight when he reined in at the Hobart yard, a good five miles from where his house had stood. He had carried on a desultory feud with the Hobarts through the years and they were barely on speaking terms. But now he sent his long, cracked cry across the yard and saw a light come up beyond the lower windows and heard Dave Hobart's sleepy voice demanding who was there.

They listened to his story in heavy silence, two part-grown girls staying in fright in the deep shadows while Margaret bathed his face and smeared grease on the worst of the cuts.

"They were here," Hobart said. He was a small man with a sharp nose and squinty blue eyes. "I understand they burned out Clymore over on Elm Creek day before yesterday. Where's it going to end?"

No one answered. No one knew.

Moss straightened from Mrs. Hobart's ministrations. "Where will I find Mitch Barton?"

They looked at him and he read the quick suspicion in their eyes and his natural sullenness threatened to take over. But it was offset by his rage at Kodyke and he railed at them.

"You think I want to turn him in? You think I'm after that ten thousand dollars gold? You're wrong. I admit I ain't been much of a neighbor. I never could get along with people somehow, but I never turned a man in for a bounty."

Hobart's voice was dry, without conviction. "So why do you want to know?"

"To join him, that's why. I never was one of the Night Riders. My place is like yours, up on the bench. The dirt they wash down didn't give me much trouble except at bad flood time, and I didn't have much to fight for."

Margaret Hobart was a resolute woman, far stronger as to character than her husband. "So what have you got to fight for now?"

Moss turned his red-veined eyes up to her. "Nothing, ma'am. I got nothing left. That coyote even took my horse, damn him, but a man has to have something or he may as well lay down and die."

She studied his face, misshapen by the cuts and bruises, then she said slowly, "We don't know where Barton is. We don't want to know. I got two girls." She indicated her watching daughters with a wave of her hand. "And while I feel the fight is right I ain't sending Hobart into it, not yet."

Moss shrugged hopelessly. "I'll find him."

"Wait," she said. "You have to eat and sleep. I'll fix something. Hobart, get him a blanket, he can sleep in the barn."

The morning sun was warm on Moss's back as he turned out of the Hobart yard. He rode a horse, a spavined gray nearly ten years old but still a better mount than the pack mule. Across the saddle he carried a shotgun. Hobart had but one rifle and no revolver, but he gave what he had.

Past noon Moss crossed the bridge and entered Morgan's Ferry. He still had no idea where Barton might be found but Hobart had said, "If it was me, I'd talk to Cap Ayres."

The street drowsed under the afternoon heat and what people were abroad stayed prudently beneath the shelter of the wooden awnings.

No one paid much attention to him as he passed. They were

too used to seeing hill ranchers ride in, their clothes ragged or carelessly patched, their horses poor, their faces drawn and gaunt with long hunger and privation.

The gray halted thankfully before the Oriental Saloon and Joe Moss stepped down, looping the reins over the rotting hitch rail, crossing the worn wooden sidewalk and pushing open the batwing doors.

He was surprised to see that the long room beyond was empty save for the bartender.

He was not a regular visitor to the saloon. For that matter, he was not a regular visitor to the town. He had neither the money for liquor or cards nor the desire for human companionship.

The bartender glanced up from the high stool on which he perched, seeing the shabby figure, the marred, swollen face, the shotgun carried loosely in Moss's left hand. He slid off the stool, coming forward not quite willingly.

"What'll you have?"

Joe Moss wet his cracked lips. He would have liked nothing so much as a drink, but his pockets were empty. The can he had used to hoard such bits of cash as came his way was buried somewhere in the ash heap of his burned house.

"To see Cap Ayres."

The bartender hesitated. "Cap's busy."

"He'll see me." Moss spoke with more confidence than he actually felt. He gestured a little with the shotgun.

The bartender was nervous. It was a nervousness which hung like a pall over the whole valley, a distrust, an uneasiness, the oppressive lull which deadens air before an approaching storm. He moved to the office door beyond the rear end of the bar. He knocked. He opened it a crack. He said something Moss could not hear, then Cap Ayres appeared, looking heavier than usual, squatter, his hook gleaming like a polished question mark in the dull light.

For a long moment he studied the man on the other side of

the bar. Then he motioned with the hook toward the cluster of deserted poker tables at the rear.

Moss followed him, never taking his eyes from the needle-like point of the hook. The shining steel fascinated him, almost hypnotized him. He remembered the stories he'd heard of how Cap had used it in barroom fights. He shuddered.

Cap Ayres saw the shudder. He was accustomed to the effect his hook had on people, nor was he above using it as a psychological advantage.

He did not know Moss although he was certain he had seen him. It was seldom that Cap forgot a face, and the fact that the man bore the marks of a savage beating roused his curiosity.

"You wanted to see me?"

Joe Moss glanced around hesitantly. The bartender had retreated to his high stool and picked up a tattered newspaper which he endeavored to read through steel-rimmed spectacles.

"I want to find Mitch Barton."

"Why?" Cap Ayres' voice held no surprise.

Joe Moss touched his warped face. "Kodyke gave me this. They burned my house. They stole my horse." The loss of the horse troubled him more than the house, for it had been a good animal, about the most valuable thing he had ever owned.

Cap's expression was suddenly hard. "You wouldn't be interested in ten thousand dollars?"

Moss did not pretend to misunderstand. "I told Kodyke I didn't like blood money. That's when he hit me."

"And what did you do then?"

"I cut his horse with my ax. The horse threw him and he pistol-whipped me."

The pistol-whipping was very plain but still Cap Ayres mistrusted the man. There was that about Joe Moss which bred a lack of confidence.

"Who sent you here?"

"Dave Hobart. He sent a note." Moss fumbled through his

pocket and handed Ayres a scrawl written on a piece of torn sacking.

Cap read it in silence. He read it twice, then he said, "Come into the office. But if you try to sell us out we'll hunt you down and hang you on a slow rope. Remember that."

CHAPTER EIGHT

JOE MOSS STARED around Cap Ayres' office in quick amazement. Eleven men were in the small room, including Cap. They studied him as he came in, their eyes neutral yet wary, and he guessed that they were here on the same errand which had brought him to Morgan's Ferry, that they had come hunting a way to join Mitch Barton and his Night Riders.

Cap's voice was dry. "A new recruit. They burned him out yesterday."

Moss knew that he was being measured, weighed, judged. The inspection made him jumpy, turned him surly, but for once he held his bitter tongue. The look in these faces frightened him more than Kodyke had.

These men had been pushed past all endurance. The hope, the caring had been squeezed out of them. They were in some respects hardly human beings any longer. Nor were they friends between themselves, for Moss saw the side glances as they regarded each other. There was only one thing to bind them together: Mitch Barton's name.

Not all of them had even known Barton and with the single exception of Cap Ayres none had been his personal friend. Yet he had become a symbol, a rallying point of mystic strength. He had escaped Kruger's men, escaped prison, and as long as he was free in the hills they could cherish a faint hope that some day the blight which had ruined their property and their lives would be swept away.

Ayres said, "We'll stay in here until full dark, then someone will lead you out."

Moss asked instinctively, "Out where?" and wished at once that he had not spoken.

Cap turned on him. The others tightened the circle, hemming him in.

"Why do you want to know?" It was Ayres. He raised the hook, polishing it lovingly with his right hand.

Moss's eyes locked on it. His throat contracted. He could feel the cold needle point against his jugular vein.

"For God sake." The words burst out of him. "I didn't mean anything, Cap. A man likes to know where he's at."

Cap wiped the hook along his shirt sleeve. "Sometimes it's safer not to know. If you ride with us you'll take orders, you won't ask questions." He broke off for the door from the barroom was opened a crack to admit the bartender's frightened face.

"Kodyke. Five men with him. He's asking for you."

Ayres turned around slowly, a pinched, gray look about his mouth. "All right. You men stay quiet. If he finds you here there'll be hell to pay."

He walked out to the barroom, closing the office door behind him. Kodyke was leaning on the bar. His men ranged behind him fan-shaped, as if expecting trouble.

Ayres nodded without speaking. Kodyke's voice was easy.

"I'm looking for Mitch Barton."

"Sorry."

The head of the mine police said pleasantly, "We expected you'd be difficult." He drew the gun from his belt, a motion so fast that Ayres' eye could not follow, and put a bullet into the ground-glass mirror of the backbar.

Cap Ayres looked at the shattered glass, stunned. It had been his pride. The backbar had been brought around the Horn in the 1850s. He turned, his face draining to ugly white.

He brought up the hook in an instinctive gesture but stopped, for Kodyke's gun was pointing directly at his broad chest.

"You might as well talk, old man. You'll be glad to before we finish with you. Where's Barton?"

Cap Ayres did not consider himself an old man. True, he had been through the war, and that was ten years past, but he was still in his middle forties. He merely shook his head.

"All right," said Kodyke. "Wreck the place."

His crew went to it with a will. They heaved over the bar. They swept the bottles from the shelves. They dumped the coal stove in the corner and were smashing the poker tables methodically when the door from Cap's office suddenly burst open. Eleven grim-faced men sprang through it, guns drawn, and Joe Moss was in the lead holding the old shotgun ready.

What might have happened had not Cap Ayres jumped in front of his friends is problematical, for one shot would have doused the saloon into flaming carnage.

"Hold it!"

Cap's sharp cry stopped every movement in the room, freezing them all motionless. One of Kodyke's men held a chair above his head. He had been ready to bring it down on the faro layout.

Kodyke had already swung his gun around and his eyes glittered with purpose. There were four unfired shells in the cylinder and he had every confidence that he could drop four men before he himself was shot. But not a dozen. And his crew's guns were in their holsters. They would have little chance of living through a first barrage. He held his fire and flung his order out.

"Put down those guns."

Cap Ayres laughed. There was hatred in the sound, and eagerness and a hungry need for action.

"Kodyke," he said, "your string has run out. You overplayed your heavy hand. No one in this room is afraid of you now. They have nothing more to lose. Fear is bred of owner-

58 / THE NIGHT RIDERS

ship, of property and the need to protect it. They've got nothing left and now neither have I."

He raised the hook in a sweeping, suggestive gesture. "Get out of here while you can still walk, and if you come again to the Ferry bring enough men to back your play. Get out."

The words broke the immobility of the scene. The man who held the chair lowered it gently to the floor as if afraid that any haste on his part would loose the crash of guns.

Kodyke hesitated an instant only. Then he dropped the black pistol into its holster and said to Ayres in his flat voice, "This is not the end of it, old man."

"No," said Ayres. "Not the end. The beginning."

He watched them go. The men behind him held their semicircle, their fingers hungry on the tight triggers.

Joe Moss said bitterly, "Why didn't we kill them?"

Cap looked at him, looked at them all. He said mildly, "And what would that accomplish? Kruger would only hire another gunman, would only double his police."

"At least it would even things for what Kodyke has done to us."

"Revenge," said Cap. "It is sweet at times I will admit, and I've lost more than you." He surveyed the wreckage of his saloon. "But think a minute. Had we killed them we'd all be on the run. As it is we're still free to ride where we choose without arguing with the law. That part is important. Mitch Barton can't ride and some of the men with him can't because the prison is hanging over them."

Joe Moss's expression was dour and others shared his doubt. "Why does the law have to be on their side? They burned my place, they beat me, yet they are free to ride."

"Because Kruger is behind them. Because Kruger has bought the courts and the law. We have to fight with what we've got. It's no good crying of justice unless we keep justice alive."

He turned quietly to the bartender. "Clean up the mess and close the doors."

THE NIGHT RIDERS / 59

The man looked at him, troubled. "Where are you going?"

"Where do you think?" Cap Ayres' grin was wide and cold. "To join Mitch Barton. I should have ridden before but I figured I had too much to lose. Kodyke has done me a favor. He's wiped away my only cause for staying."

CHAPTER NINE

DUNKIN HASKELL and his two partners had prospected a quartz outcropping in a box canyon dug like a deep heelprint into the side of Doan Mountain.

The discovery had been made in '58. In '61 they had sold out to a crowd of San Francisco financiers, and these had spent an even million dollars carving out a road through the inaccessible country, driving a haulage tunnel a mile into the heart of the mountain.

But the vein which had been astonishingly wide at the surface narrowed as the tunnel followed it, and finally pinched out altogether. The property was abandoned. The shelflike road dug into the canyon side at such great expense caved with the action of the frost, in spots was buried by slides from above, all but obliterated. It was now impassable. The only remaining way into the canyon was a narrow, tortuous trail by which Haskell and his partners had entered originally.

It was down this trail's sharp switchbacks that Cap Ayres led his party to join the riders who had already found their way to Mitch Barton.

Barton stood now in the doorway of the long log mess hall of the old mine. When it was raised there were better than two hundred workmen in the canyon, and some fifty buildings had made the irregular pattern of a town. Most of these houses were in sad repair. The peeled pine walls still stood but the mud chinking had fallen away and half the roofs had collapsed under the tremendous weight of the winter snows.

It was cold in the thin air and Cap Ayres' breath made visible wispy smoke as he came wearily off his horse, handing the reins to Moss and walking to where Barton watched their arrival.

"How's it going?"

Mitch Barton shrugged and there was reserve in his words. "Not too good. Only twenty men so far." He looked at those who had followed Cap into the valley and the corners of his mouth turned down.

Cap saw the look. Barton roused himself as if his thoughts had not been in the canyon but a thousand miles away. He motioned to Emmett Foster, telling him to show the newcomers where to put their horses, where to bunk, and then to take them to the shack which had been turned into a cook house. And when Foster had gone he touched the saloon man's arm and led him inside the old mess hall.

One end of the big building still had a serviceable roof. The room had been cleared of the debris which a hundred generations of pack rats had happily deposited on its sagging floor. A bunk had been built along one wall and a trestle table dragged beneath the shelter.

Cap judged that Mitch Barton used it as an office. He sat down on the foot of the bunk, his big body drooping with tiredness. He pulled his hat from his head and used his hook to scratch above one ear. Barton watched him with distaste.

"Sometime you're going to run that pig stabber into your own throat."

Cap smiled wryly. "You'd be surprised how it impresses people. Even Kodyke doesn't enjoy the idea of the thing."

Barton said in dissatisfaction, "I thought you were going to stay down in the valley, to be our eyes and ears."

"No use." Cap shrugged. He went on to tell of the saloon's destruction. "Kodyke's playing right into your lap," he said.

"Half the men who rode in with me wouldn't have come if he'd left them alone. Even Joe Moss is ready to fight now."

"Who's he?"

"A hill rancher, hardscrabble, a rawhider." Cap used the terms of contempt with which the larger ranchers referred to their improvident neighbors. "He had no real fight with Kruger and the mines. His ranch, for what it's worth, isn't much affected by the flooding and the silt, but Kodyke burned him out because he called the reward offered for your recapture blood money. By the way, it's gone up."

"Gone up?"

"There were notices posted in the sheriff's office yesterday. Ten thousand dollars gold for the man who brings you in, dead or alive."

Mitch Barton's mouth twisted. "If they get it high enough I might claim it myself. I don't seem to be doing much good here."

"As bad as that?"

Barton's laugh was cruel. "Carl Dill thought the valley would rise en masse when they heard I was free. Well, they haven't." His voice held the bitter edge of disillusionment. "We've all been fools, all been kidding ourselves."

Cap Ayres sighed. "Mitch, you were away for a long time. A lot of the men we'll have to depend on grew up while you weren't here. Those who once rode with you are older, much older, they've lost hope. Those who aren't dead. What you need is to move. So far Kodyke and his crew are in control, everybody's afraid of them. You'll have to hit the mines and hit hard. Then, when you've done that, we'll have more volunteers than we can handle."

Mitch Barton looked at him, his lips a sour line curving more in self-mockery than amusement.

"The old story, which comes first, the chicken or the egg. I can't hit Kruger hard enough to do any good without sufficient men and I can't get the men until I've made a play."

Cap Ayres was silent. Barton picked up a twig from the floor and broke it sharply.

"Dill still says the valley will rally to us. He doesn't think we should move too fast. He claims that if we strike without enough force and are beaten we'll not only fail to recruit fresh men but those we have will drift away."

Ayres was stubborn. "I don't trust Dill." His voice was thick with dislike. "The man's a thief. He worked for Kruger and did his dirty work and all the time he was stealing from the mines. Now he hates Kruger for catching him. He isn't fighting for the valley. He's fighting because he's a bad loser."

"So long as he fights." Mitch Barton sounded indifferent.

Cap had watched the man unhappily and he said now, "You've changed a lot, Mitch. Bitterness has dulled the spark that made people listen to you."

"What do you expect?"

Cap rose. "I'll not quarrel with you," he said and walked heavily out of the hall into the warming sunlight, leaving Barton to glower after him with smouldering eyes.

Beyond the broken doorway Cap paused to look over the rotting community. In the few days since the escapees had moved in there had been much change wrought in the old mine village. Someone had brought quick order to the ruined place. A pole corral of straight young pines, their mottled bark glowing red in the morning light, had been built along the grassy bank of the clear and rushing creek. Within it half a hundred horses circled the enclosure slowly. Tables had been hauled from the old mess building, cleaned and lined up in the open beside the cook shack. There the men who had ridden in with him were already eating, wearing off the edge of their sharp hunger.

High on the rim above the old mine tunnel a spotter patrolled among the rocks that hid him from outside view, and Cap knew that nothing could move in the country below without being seen. Even if Kodyke discovered the hideout they would have ample time, ample warning of an attack.

He nodded in satisfaction at the physical shape of the camp, but he was uneasy with Barton's frame of mind. He sighed and started toward the cook shack, then paused, for Marie Beauchamp had called his name.

He turned quickly, seeing her standing in the doorway of a cabin set somewhat apart from the rest. This was larger than the others, the superintendent's home during the years of the mine's operation, and in better condition, for the caretaker had used it before the company finally abandoned the property.

He crossed toward her, stiff-legged from his unaccustomed all-night ride, and put out his good hand which she caught in both of hers.

"Cap, it's good to see you. Come in. I was just about to go absolutely crazy."

He held back a moment. "And I was just about to go eat while the food's still hot."

"I'll feed you here," she said and pulled him against his will into the big front room.

His quick glance showed the place spotlessly clean. She had even found some bright material, forgotten on the shelves of the company store, and rigged a semblance of curtains for the windows. He caught his breath, surprised at what she had managed with so little.

"Where's the Tiger?"

Her mouth formed a tight, suddenly angry line. "Down by the creek fishing, I think, or watching the horses or the men. I hardly see him from sunrise until dark."

He sank into a rawhide chair. The leather had cracked and broken in half a dozen places and she had repaired it with knotted rope. She moved to the stove in the corner and thrust chunks of deadfall wood into it, stirring the fire to quick new life.

"Steak and beans."

He raised his eyebrows and she moved her shoulders. "Oh, we have enough to eat, I'll give Carl Dill that. The man's mind is like a machine and he planned this thing months ago. There

64 / THE NIGHT RIDERS

are thirty head of cattle below the falls at the lower end of the canyon, and he must have made fifty pack trips up here with supplies."

She turned back to the stove, its gathering heat bringing a rose flush to her cheeks. He thought again how like a little girl she was, and something mounted in him that would not subside.

Cap Ayres was not a soft man. He had come off an Ohio farm at sixteen. He had fought in the First Battle of Bull Run, and had been with Sherman in the march to the sea. Then he had come West, conscious of the hook that took the place of his lost left hand, choosing for companions women on the back streets of the towns, never intruding on what he considered the better elements of the communities.

Marie Beauchamp was a new experience for him. He had offered her help at first because of Mitch Barton's son. He had known that she was a gambler and had rated her in his mind accordingly. But then something had happened to him. He had fallen in love with her. He was not a man who evaded, he met his emotions head on and spent no time in self-justification. Six months ago he had asked her to marry him, asked it with the intensity of a middle-aged man who feels that life has nearly passed him by.

He had not been surprised at her refusal, but he had been amazed with her gentleness. She had laid a small hand on his arm and her black eyes had held a softness which he had never caught there before.

"You're the best friend I've had, Cap, about the only one. Let's not spoil something so good with something that would not be honest."

"Meaning that you couldn't love me?"

"I've never loved any man that way. Perhaps it's a lack in me, or maybe it was because I idolized my father to the point where no one I meet ever measures up. Can't we let things go on as they are?"

He had doubted it. He had expected strain between them,

but he had not counted on the girl. She had a way of confiding in him, of sharing her problems with him that had drawn them closer even than they had been before.

Cap Ayres watched her now as she placed the meat in the pan, and the sizzling of it filled the room, mingling with the odor of fresh-boiled coffee. When the steaks were done she ladled out beans from the iron pot and pulled biscuits from the stove, then, setting them before him, she took the stool on the other side of the table.

"Go ahead and eat."

He ate with the single-minded intentness of a very hungry man, and she remained silent, understanding. Not until he had finished, had shoved back his plate and drawn the blackened pipe from his pocket did she speak.

"Can Barton win this fight?"

He took time to ignite the tobacco, watching her through the curling smoke. "You don't want him to win, do you?"

She spread her hands in a quick flutter. "I don't care. It means nothing to me."

He said shrewdly, "You've never lied to me, Marie. Don't start now."

Her eyes sharpened and some of the softness disappeared from their depths. "Why should I want him to lose?"

"Because he stands between you and the boy. Because if he wins, if he gets his legal freedom he will take his son away from you. You're already objecting that the child is fishing, enjoying the horses and the men, being drawn into the new life."

She was silent and by her silence giving confirmation to his words. Finally she said, "It's the first childhood he's had. Of course I want him to have it, if Barton weren't the one to give it."

"You really hate him, don't you?"

She said slowly, distinctly, "I have never really hated anyone else in my life. Shall I tell you why?"

Cap Ayres shook his head. "I don't want to hear it, Marie."

"Hear it anyway." Her voice rose on a note of hysteria. "My sister had a voice, a great voice. From the moment our father died I worked for enough money to take her to Italy for the training she deserved.

"And then Mitchell Barton came to San Francisco. To try to reason with Kruger." She laughed, a short, hard sound. "He met Lucy in the hotel lobby. Three days later he married her. Without a word to me. He didn't tell her he was in trouble. She knew nothing about the fight in the valley until they came back to Morgan's Ferry and he was arrested for dynamiting those water ditches."

"Which he did not do."

"The court said he did. He was in prison when the baby came, when she died in childbirth. And now he wants to take the boy away from me too."

She was gripping the edge of the table until her knuckles showed white beneath the skin. "I'll kill him before I give Ralph up. I'll kill him."

Ayres shook his head. "No you won't."

She stared at him as if he were a stranger, then she said in a quieter tone, "Make him let me take the boy away, Cap. Suppose Kodyke finds us here. Suppose Ralph is killed."

He was silent and she stood up slowly, fighting herself for control. "Listen to me, Cap. You know me well enough to know I don't make idle threats. If he doesn't let me take the boy East I'll turn every man in this camp against him."

Cap Ayres' eyes were on her, filled with the knowledge of a lifetime spent in watching people from behind a bar. It was his axiom that you could tell more about a man after a second drink than from knowing him for years. And Marie Beauchamp was drunk on her emotion.

"I hope you know what you're doing."

"If you mean, do I know men, I certainly do. I was raised in a gambling house, remember. I have no respect nor trust for any of them, but I can handle them, I can use them. Never worry about me."

CHAPTER TEN

MITCH BARTON AND CARL DILL were standing at the head of the long table when Cap Ayres joined them. The men who had ridden in with Ayres were still eating, the others gathered around with worried questions about conditions in the valley.

Barton turned as the saloon man came up, saying, "Get yourself a plate."

Cap gave him a thin-lipped smile. "I just dined, in far handsomer company."

Barton glanced automatically toward the girl's cabin and the corners of his eyes showed tiny wrinkles as he frowned.

"I'm glad." His tone showed that he was not. "You and I need to talk." As he spoke he was conscious of the petulance that came over Carl Dill's face. It was as if the ex-auditor resented Cap's presence and his close association with Barton.

It could be mere jealousy if Dill, savoring his place as Barton's lieutenant, resented the idea that Ayres might usurp his privilege, or it could be that Dill had some buried plan of his own. Prison had sharpened Mitch Barton's perceptions and virtually killed his trust in his fellow men. Behind the walls you had to be on constant guard, he felt, for there were few inmates who would not sell out their companions to curry a breath of favor with the authorities.

Barton glanced at Cap and saw that the one-armed man was watching Dill, not troubling to hide his dislike, so that neither was surprised when Dill jibed, "Didn't expect to find you here, Ayres. I didn't know you had any fighting blood left."

Ayres' voice was dangerously soft. "What makes you say that?"

68 / THE NIGHT RIDERS

Dill's shrug was elaborate. "During the time I was arranging for Barton's escape you refused to lift a finger."

Ayres said flatly, "I just don't trust thieves."

Red came up into Dill's face and his fists knotted at his sides. For an instant Barton thought he would strike the saloon owner and set himself, knowing that if the blow was passed Cap would go into quick action with his murderous hook.

But Dill managed to check himself, then spun and strode away from the table and someone laughed, too loudly, nervously.

Barton looked sharply from the retreating Dill to the other, took Ayres' arm and led him out of earshot of the group and spoke in an undertone.

"Save your fighting for Donald Kruger. What's wrong between you and Dill?"

Cap shrugged. "We just don't see things the same way. I have no faith in his sincerity and he knows it."

Mitch Barton had a deep belief in the saloon man's judgment. Of all the men at the old mine he held Ayres in highest esteem, yet he was moved to protest.

"I wouldn't be free if it weren't for Dill. I shared a cell with him for a long time, and you get to know a man pretty well in prison."

"Do you like him?"

Mitch Barton hesitated, considering carefully before he answered. He knew that he had been drawn to Dill by the man's obvious hatred of Donald Kruger, and that most of their conversations had concerned the mining king and Dill's plans for revenge.

"I owe him a great deal . . ." He said it doggedly.

"I didn't ask that."

"No . . . Can I put it this way then. If I were going to choose a friend, Dill would not be the first I would select."

Cap spat thoughtfully on the flinty ground between his feet. "And what about me?"

"You?" Barton felt a shock at the question. "I never gave

that much thought. Yes, you're a friend, one I would choose immediately."

"All right," said Ayres, and looked at Barton's eyes. "I had to know, because I'm going to ask you a favor, now. Send Marie and the child away."

Barton stepped back, and his voice was puzzled. "I thought we'd been all over that at the Ferry. I don't dare send him away, Cap. If Kruger ever got his hands on my boy . . ."

"That was at the Ferry. Here it is different. I can get them across the mountains and put them on a train for the East at Reno Junction from here."

"She's been working on you, hasn't she?"

Dull color rose under the heavy tan of Cap's face. "Nobody needs to work on me, Barton. And this is no set-up for a woman or a kid. You know it yourself."

Barton suddenly almost laughed. "How long have you been in love with her?"

Cap swung away in quick withdrawal but Barton reached out a hand to catch his arm.

"All right." His tone had changed, grown brisk and somehow relaxed. "We've got to do something and do it fast. Your idea is what?"

Before Ayres could answer a call from the crest came down through the mountain air and they raised their eyes together to the mine shaft and the guard stationed there a thousand feet above them.

"Someone's coming."

At once the whole camp was alert. Men who had been eating idly seized their guns and spread out to places of shelter. Mitch Barton made no attempt to hide, but with Cap watched the waving arms of the signaling figure.

"A single rider."

They waited in silence for what seemed hours, watching the horseman come over the crest, watching the guard slip down from his vantage point to his horse's side, out of sight, and then seeing the newcomer drop on down the sharp switchbacks of the trail as it skirted the breast of the mine dump.

Cap recognized him long before he reached the floor of the bowl.

"That's one of Al Hammond's boys. Hammond's been working up at the Ione pit. He said he'd send word if there was anything we should know."

The boy was young, in his early teens. His hair was flaxen, turned lighter by constant exposure to the raw sun, and he was feeling important, sensing that the news he bore was weighty. He spoke even before he stepped tiredly from the saddle.

"Kruger's at the mine."

The men had come out of their hiding places, gaunt, grim-faced men, their clothes showing the stress of age. They stared at the boy, turning his news over in their minds.

"At Ione?" Carl Dill had pressed forward until he stood at Barton's elbow. "You mean he actually came up to the valley himself? . . . Then we've got him worried. He hasn't been up here in years."

Barton was studying the boy. "Did you see him?"

The youngster nodded.

"Did he seem worried?"

"Well, he was mad. I heard him bawling out Mr. Hague and Kodyke. I only saw him for about a minute, and then they all went into the office."

"When did he get there?"

The boy didn't know.

"How long is he going to stay?"

The boy didn't know that either.

Barton raised his head to the men and a brief, chill smile touched his straight lips. "This might be the break we're looking for."

They watched him, eagerness rising in their bearded faces. Inaction was the hardest thing they had had to bear, and any move was better than sitting in the desolate valley waiting for they knew not what.

"If we can con Kodyke and his police away, perhaps we can talk to Kruger."

"Talk to him?" The words burst from Carl Dill. "Talk to him hell. If we can catch him without his guards we can kill him."

Barton's head jerked around and he glared coldly at the man.

"We are not murderers. We are not seeking revenge. Justice is what we're after, and we won't get it by killing Kruger. And I'm not just being soft. I hate the man as thoroughly as you do, but even if he died the mines would continue to operate, until we prove to the state that we need the protection of law to stop their abuses."

Dill's lip curled. "I thought you were more realistic. They'd shoot you down like a mongrel if they had the slightest chance."

Barton shrugged. There was no point in arguing with Dill.

"What about the rest of you?"

Kid Boyd grinned. "You're the boss."

"All right then. I'll take Cap and two men with me. We'll ride to the mine. If we leave now we should be there by midnight. Foster, you and the rest ride up and cut the main ditch two miles above the mine. They probably have guards posted all along the line. Don't ride into a trap."

Dill was surly. "What good will that do?"

"The minute the water ceases to reach the monitors Kodyke and his gang are going out to learn why. The minute they leave, Cap and I can drop in for a little talk with Kruger." He turned slowly, singling out Rankin and Kid Boyd. "You two stay here, one on the lookout and one in camp."

They nodded silently.

"Okay, get your horses." He looked at the cook. "Give each man a chunk of meat and some cold biscuits." He swung away then and walked hurriedly down toward the creek where it ran in its boulder-strewn course along the base of the cliff.

Ralph Barton sat on a rock in the shade of a stunted pine, a four-foot aspen pole in his small hands and three trout

72 / **THE NIGHT RIDERS**

hoarded beside him. Against the noisy rush of the stream he neither heard nor sensed his father's approach until Mitch's shadow fell across the slight shoulders. Then he looked up and grinned. The change in the boy was amazing to the man who had watched it come day by day. The sun and wind had fully erased the pallor of indoor living and tanned the smooth face to an even brown. But the change went far deeper than sunburn. The shy grin itself was indication that the child had relaxed, had put away the dead-pan mask with which he had faced the players across the faro bank.

"Hi, Dad. Look at my fish."

"Keep on and you'll be feeding the whole crew." Barton squatted down. As he did so there was a sharp tug at the line and they were tensely still while the boy brought in a ten-inch flashing trout.

He held it up in shining pride and Barton felt a surge of warmth in his chest. He had known small love in his life. His mother had died before he could remember and his father had been largely a remote man, undemonstrative. Only for the few short days of his marriage before his arrest had he known the communication of love. Impulsively he reached out and put his arm about the boy, but he felt the small figure stiffen and unself-consciously draw away. At once he dropped his arm, saying lightly, "I'm riding. Take care of the camp until I get back."

The boy's head came around and the dark eyes with their curling lashes widened.

"Are you going to blow up the mine now?" There was a note of accusation in the tone which brought a flush, hot under Barton's new-found tan.

"Not exactly," he said. "I'm going up to see the man who has caused all this trouble. I'm going to straighten it out."

"Aunt Marie says you're going to blow up the ditches and probably get yourself killed."

Anger against the girl rose in Mitch Barton and for a moment harsh words trembled on his lips. Then he stilled them

THE NIGHT RIDERS / 73

with an almost physical effort. The boy needed her, no matter how much he himself despised the Yankee Duchess.

He shook his head. "I'm not going to get killed. Now, you take care of the camp." He said the last a little lamely and reluctantly headed back toward the mine buildings.

Marie Beauchamp had just put new-made bread into her oven to bake. She planned to invite Cap Ayres for dinner and was arranging in her mind the arguments she meant to use to try to get the saloon man to help her in taking the boy away. When the knock rattled the door she somehow assumed that it was Ayres and called pleasantly, "Come in."

Mitch Barton pushed open the door and stood for a moment framed in the entrance, caught unaware by the good smell of the bread and the friendly voice, and the quick sight of the girl. She had turned from the stove, her face flushed by the heat and her dark hair damp against her forehead, forming natural curls. Her eyes were bright with the expectation of seeing Ayres.

They darkened, dulled as she realized who was there and resentment rose in her like a pillar of mounting fire.

"What do you want?"

They had not exchanged more than a hundred words since coming to the camp and the tension between them was a live thing, filling the room as his moment of warmth passed.

He said tonelessly, "We're riding out. I'm leaving guards. Do not try to run away. If you haven't sense enough to realize the dangers in the hills I'm telling you. Kodyke's men are still searching for us. If they found you and Ralph I doubt that you would both survive."

He stood yet a moment, undecided, as if not knowing how to say good-by, and when the woman did not answer he backed out, slamming the door.

"The bitch." He thought of her as the most cold-blooded person he had ever known. He was still shaking with his automatic anger as he mounted his horse and led the party up the switchbacks of the old trail.

Cap Ayres was riding at his side. Cap had observed him come from the cabin and knew him well enough to gauge the inner tumult which Barton struggled to control.

"Why don't you let her leave?" Cap said softly.

Barton glanced at him sharply, then back at the trailing men. The closest rider was a good thirty feet behind.

"How can I? She wouldn't leave without the boy and I'm damned if I'll let her run off with him."

"Are you sure you'd want to see her go anyhow?"

"What are you getting at?"

Cap scratched the stubble on his jaw with the curve of his hook.

"I don't rightly know. I'm no authority on human emotions, but I've found that sometimes when two people appear to hate each other the way you and the Duchess do, there's something behind it."

"I don't know what you mean."

"Maybe you're afraid of each other. I know the girl pretty well, better than I've known any other woman. I love her. She likes me and trusts me. That I know, and she is not one who gives her trust easily."

Barton was silent, edgy.

"But she won't marry me. And I've watched her face when she talks about you. I think you're both fighting an attraction that neither will admit to."

Barton's laugh was short and bitter. "You're as romantic as a gabbling fishwife Say what you've just said here to Marie Beauchamp and see her reaction. She hates me as much as any individual can possibly hate another. And it's mutual."

He kicked his horse ahead against the sharpness of the rising grade, and Ayres let him go, shaking his head ruefully.

"I'm a fool," he thought. "Whatever hope I had is gone now. The idea is in his head. He'll fight it like the stubborn man he is. But sooner or later he will know the truth, and I hope it happens in time."

CHAPTER ELEVEN

Alone in the cabin Marie Beauchamp stood at the window, her tight fist holding the chintz curtain barely open, watching the men ride out, the excited wheeling of the horses, the noisy confusion as the men found their saddles and circled for position, and then the roiling cloud of choking dust as the grim column formed and stretched along the trail and was ominously gone.

In the sharp silence that remained behind them a crisp ring of hammer on metal was like the ghost of the recent clamor. Fred Rankin was shoeing a horse beside the corral. The cook puttered quietly around the wagon, and in a moment Ralph Barton wandered up the path from the creek carrying his string of fish.

She watched as the boy halted to talk to Rankin, noting the way the sun touched his dark hair warmly, noting the straightness of the young figure. She was a woman born to deep emotion, who had repressed it almost from childhood as if she failed to trust herself. She had idolized her gambler father and set herself to pattern her existence after his, and when he had died she had dedicated herself and all of her efforts toward raising her younger sister, toward cultivating the voice for which her father had had such hopes. As her father had planned, she worked toward a glorious career for Lucy.

She would never, she knew, forget the feeling of unbelieving shock she had experienced that morning when her sister and Barton had appeared at her rooms to announce that they were married. Her world as she had pictured it collapsed in that moment, and the sister who had meant everything was suddenly a stranger removed from her, both small hands on the arm of the big male figure, eyes turned upward in pride to his, pride and trust, never seeing the anguish that contorted Marie's face.

The Duchess closed her lips tightly against the memory, trying to compose herself, for the boy was now coming on toward the cabin.

He danced in gaily, swinging the fish importantly.

"Look." He held them under her nose. "Father said that if I kept on I'd be feeding the whole crew."

She took them from him jealously, as if Barton had a part in them, and carried them to the iron sink in the corner where water brought through a wooden trough from halfway up the mountain ran constantly out of a section of rusted pipe.

"They're beautiful. Come and give me a kiss." She schooled her voice, put the fish aside and crouched to take him into her arms. "Do you like it here, Ralph?"

He grinned. "It's great."

"I saw you stop to talk to Mr. Rankin. Do you like him?"

"Sure, he's swell. He fixed my pole last week. Is he a gunfighter, Marie?" He had never called her Aunt.

"I don't know." She was startled. "Where did you hear that?"

"Some of the men were talking. They said he was sent to prison for killing a man."

She had not known this and it gave her pause, but she felt that she had little choice. Kid Boyd, left on guard, was an old friend of Barton's and idolized the leader. She knew that she could never persuade him to enter into her plot. And the cook was hopeless. It left Rankin as her only resort. She thought it over carefully. She had little fear of men. She had been around them in the gambling houses since her sixteenth birthday and had always been able to avoid trouble.

"I don't know about it." She made the words easy. "Maybe he had good reason to. You don't know the full story."

The boy brightened and Marie smiled.

"Do you like him well enough to ask him if he wants to eat these fish with us?"

"Why, yes." It was a new idea. "Shall I ask him now?"

She nodded. "Tell him that I have some fresh bread too, that lunch will be ready in about thirty minutes."

She released him and watched him hurry off. Then quickly she turned to the alcove and the peg which held the only other dress she had in camp, the evening costume she had worn when Barton had taken them from Cap Ayres' place. She struggled into it, arranged her hair before the blighted mirror, and tying a towel about her, went back to the sink and began to clean the fish.

Fred Rankin was paring the horse's hoof. He turned to the fire in the homemade forge, tested the cherry-red shoe, then with the tongs dipped it into the wooden pail of water to sizzle and steam. He was so intent on what he was doing that he was unaware of Ralph Barton's return until the boy spoke.

"My aunt wants you to come and eat my trout with us."

Rankin almost dropped the shoe in surprise, but after a moment he masked his amazement and went on with his job, driving the nails expertly into the hoof one after the other, clipping the ends and clinching them in place. Not until he had finished and turned the fresh-shod animal back into the corral and refastened the pole gate did he answer. Then he turned around.

"How come?"

The boy shrugged. "Well, she saw me talking to you and she asked if I liked you and I said sure, you fixed my fish pole. And then she said maybe you'd like to eat trout with us."

Fred Rankin considered. Experience had made him a careful man. Automatically he distrusted any action he did not understand, and he did not understand this invitation. But he had been in prison for years and Marie Beauchamp was the first woman he had been at all associated with in a long time.

He had watched her ever since coming to the camp, noting with hunger her beauty, speculating as lonely men will. He knew, as did everyone at the hideout, that she and Barton were battling. He did not know the reason and he did not care.

78 / THE NIGHT RIDERS

"Well, yes," he said and smiled, his green eyes lighting. "Tell her I'll be there as soon as I can change my shirt."

He touched the boy's shoulder then and walked off toward the bunkhouse, unrolling his other shirt, and afterward crossed to the cook shack for a bar of yellow soap.

The cook, old to the point of crankiness, watched him dourly. "You fixin' to bathe midweek?"

Rankin growled at him. "Any objections?"

The cook's answer was hasty, for Rankin's reputation was well known in camp. "None, Mr. Rankin, none. Grub will be in half an hour."

"I'm eating with Miss Beauchamp."

The cook dropped the big spoon he had been holding. He bent to pick it up and when he straightened said without expression, "You know Barton's orders. We're all to keep away from that cabin."

"Hell with Barton." Rankin swung on his heel and strode on down to the rushing creek.

Behind the shelter of a pile of rocks he stripped and plunged into the icy water, found a pebble bar and stood up to soap his muscular body, enjoying the bite of the lye on his skin. He rinsed, rolling in the shallow pool, then climbed out and stood in the warmth of the sun, letting it rob the tingling chill that quickened him. He dressed slowly, regarding the soiled, frayed pants with distaste. He had been something of a dandy before his prison days. He had known many women then, but as he slicked his red hair into place he admitted to himself that he had never known anyone like the Duchess.

The fish were brown and crisp. The bread was light, still warm from the oven and crusty, and even the beans managed to taste different from those the cook served, as if she had added some local aromatic herb.

Fred Rankin pushed his chair back from the crude table and sighed his content. Marie Beauchamp rose to gather the dishes and stack them in the sink and speak over her shoulder.

"You're welcome to smoke if you like."

He nodded, brought out the short black pipe and packed it with tobacco sliced from the dark plug, thinking that he would prefer a cigar as a better compliment to this meal. It had been a long, long time since he had had either good food or cigar.

The woman, finished at the sink, turned back to the room, smiling.

"Ralph, your fish were mighty good. Why don't you go get some more for our dinner?"

The boy looked up at her and then at Rankin. "Sure. Want to come, Fred?"

The man shook his head. "I ate too much. I'll just sit here and relax a little. Have good luck."

When the boy was gone there was a prolonged silence in the cabin. Rankin was the one who finally broke it. He took his pipe from his mouth and his voice was flat, chipped when he spoke.

"All right, what's the game?"

She started to say, "What game?" and then decided there was no point in wasting time. She looked at him squarely.

"I want to get out of here. Barton is holding Ralph and me virtual prisoners."

Rankin shrugged. "The kid is his."

"He's mine." It was a cry, a protest against the child's belonging to anyone but herself. "I raised him. Barton never saw him until the night he moved us up here."

"All right. Where do you want to go?"

"To Nevada. To some place where I can get a train for the East."

He knocked out the pipe deliberately against the stool's leg, ignoring the litter the ashes made on the floor. "What will you pay?"

She caught her breath. She had not expected him to be so matter of fact. "I have some money that I brought from Cap's saloon."

"To hell with money."

They looked at each other fully, and his eyes were more expressive than any words. A tiny shudder ran through Marie Beauchamp's small body but she was too adept at controlling her emotions to let the man see.

She said steadily, "Once we're safe at the railroad ask anything you want," and saw the light of anticipation glow for an instant in the hard face.

"I'll have to get rid of Boyd," he said, as if he said he'd have to get horses. "He's watching from the ridge. He'd stop us if we rode out."

She had not thought of that and for a moment she hesitated, then she nodded. "But don't kill him."

Rankin's thin-lipped mouth split in a small grin that held no humor.

"I don't know what you've heard about me, but I don't go around killing people just for the fun of watching them die. The only difference between me and the average man is that when I pull a gun I mean to use it."

He rose then, leisurely, and left the cabin, stalking across the hard, hot ground with as near a swagger as he ever used. Two people watched him, Marie Beauchamp from the cabin window and the cook from the shelter of the shack.

The girl was now torn by doubts, by fears. Never before in her memory had she hesitated once a decision was taken. She had lived by accepting the turn of a card. But now she almost called him back, almost told him she had changed her mind, for the thing she had seen in his green eyes had thoroughly frightened her. It was cold, and heedless of human values beyond anything she had before experienced.

The cook watched from the shadow of his shack. His old lips over his empty gums were pulled together in a grim line. He had spent most of his life on the Barton ranch, first as a rider and then after a fall had partly crippled him, as boss of the commissary. His was the fierce loyalty that the employees of the semi-feudal cattle outfits had always given to their brand. It had been so and it was so now. For him Mitch Barton was always right and those who stood against him were enemies.

He saw Rankin catch up a horse, swing into the saddle with the panther grace that characterized all the man's movements. He watched as the horse was put toward the mine dump and began the climb up the switchbacks toward where Kid Boyd squatted on the high boulder commanding the rolling country to the west.

The cook came at length out of the shadow and stood undecided, rubbing the leg of one scuffed boot. Then with hesitation he moved toward Marie Beauchamp's cabin.

Outside the doorway he stopped, breathing deeply, steeling himself for what loomed as the worst ordeal of his life. He knocked.

Inside there was a long silence. Marie Beauchamp stood staring at the door, her mind racing to discover who it might be beyond the panel. She had seen Rankin ride up the grade and she could think of no one else in camp.

She moved with quiet speed to one of the two bunks and pulled the small pearl-handled derringer from beneath her pillow. It had been her father's gun, one he had carried clipped to a holdout in his sleeve. Its small carved butt fitted neatly into her own palm, and though its four revolving barrels looked too tiny even to take their loads, when pressed against a man's stomach its strike was deadly

She held it in her right hand, partly concealed in the folds of her dress, and turned to face the door, calling from where she stood.

"Come in."

The cook pushed open the door slowly. She looked at his thin, bearded face, his red-rimmed eyes and thin white hair in relieved surprise. They had never spoken to each other but she knew at once who he was.

"Yes?"

Suddenly she felt silly holding the little gun. This man was as dangerous as an earthworm, and as obtrusive. She managed to slide the derringer into her pocket as his broken hands fumbled, twisting the brim of his worn hat. Still she watched him in curiosity. He made no effort to come forward into the room. His tongue was faded to blue with his age and he used its tip to moisten his sunken lips.

"Ma'am, I don't know how to say this . . ."

"Say what?" Her curiosity was giving way to impatience. She wanted him gone so that she could pack. Not that there was much to take, but she wanted to be ready as soon as Rankin gave a signal. She wanted to be as far from this place as she could before Barton's return.

"It's Rankin." The words burst out of the old man. "He's no good, ma'am. He's a low-down, no-account killer. I wouldn't trust him with a five-day-old sour-dough biscuit."

She had a compulsion to laugh suddenly, but she did not dare.

"Thanks," she said. "I can handle Rankin." Her tone was shorter than she intended, almost curt.

"That's what women always think." The cook was still fumbling for words. "Women always think that. The trouble is, women don't understand what makes a man tick."

She smiled, hiding the wish that he would leave without her having to send him off.

"I know," his old eyes were on her face and she almost started, seeing a shrewdness there that she had not suspected. "You hate Barton. You want to clear out with the boy and you're fixing to use Rankin to get you away."

Her silence was cautious now, and he kept talking.

"A pretty woman can get a lot out of almost any man, but she can get hurt bad too. I'd shoot him if I thought I could. There ain't much chance and I ain't got much nerve. You go get the boy. You and he can hide in the mine tunnel until Barton gets back. I know a place the devil himself couldn't find you."

She shook her head. She said, "Thanks," with lips that were strangely stiff. "I can't back out now. I've got to go on with it."

Somehow she felt lonely after he had bobbed out and closed the door. Once again her decision was taken, and she could not alter it. She turned to filling the saddlebags.

She heard Rankin's horse as it came off the mountain, heard the harsh strike of its hoofs on the sharp rocks. She went to the window and saw him at the corral gate working out his loop, catching one horse and then a second. She saw him throw the saddles on them and then move down to the creek. In a few minutes he came back with the boy and she crossed to open the door. Ralph's eyes were dark, questioning, and a little fearful.

"Fred says we're going away."

She nodded. "We're going East, honey. To Chicago, to New York, maybe to Paris. You'll like it."

The child's face got a sullen look. "I like it here."

"That's because you've never seen all the other places. Now go and change your clothes. We have a long, hard ride ahead."

He hesitated for a minute, but the habit of obedience was strong and he pushed past her into the cabin. She stepped outside, closing the door and looking up into Rankin's face.

"What happened about Boyd?" she asked in a low voice.

"He's tied up."

"You didn't hurt him?"

Rankin's eyes glowed slightly. "Not much. I had to conk him. He was giving me an argument. Come on, let's get going. I want to get to a main trail by dark."

CHAPTER TWELVE

THE ROAR OF THE MONITORS filled the night. The pounding hoses tore at the wounded mountain. It was an awesome and imposing sight, this destruction of the earth's crust by the force of water.

84 / THE NIGHT RIDERS

Man had devised many ways to rob nature of her buried riches, but never in the history of mining had he come up with as effective and inexpensive way of wrenching gold from the unwilling soil.

They stood on the lip of the hole being chewed into the heart of the bank, looking down upon the scene below them. There was a grandeur about it which even Barton felt, despite his anger. This was not the first time he had seen the monitors at work, but once again he was impressed by the ant-sized figures and their dexterity with their mighty weapons.

Mounted on the tripod standards the giant copper nozzles spit out lances of water with a force that would tear a man in two. Their masters worked with the precise care of a sculptor, undercutting a section of the cemented gravel, routing out the support of the stuff above until they dropped an avalanche carefully aimed for the great sluice box below. Here the whole slide was caught, to be churned in the cascade of water rushing to the lower level. A hundred thousand horses working together could not have duplicated that battering force.

The maw of the sluice held rows of teeth, railroad rails set on end and bedded deeply in concrete, screening out the trees, the brush and boulders. Behind this barricade the teeth drew closer together to become a grizzly which broke up the sandy clots, and these, sliding through the rails, were then washed down and through a screen, falling into yet another water-powered device, the revolving trummel.

Like a giant wire cylinder lined with heavy blades, the trummel rolled, breaking the gravels into free sand and at last releasing the black sand and fine gold particles. From the trummel the larger stones were rejected while the fines fell again, into the mile-long sluice box.

Along the riffled bottom of this trough washed the fines, a mixture of mud, of sand and of gold, and here the heavier gold settled behind the corrugated ridges while the lighter sand and mud were carried along to be dumped eventually into the steep river.

THE NIGHT RIDERS / 85

It was these fines, spewed with arrogant disregard into the natural water course, which were ruining the valley and even being carried as a blight as far southwestward as San Francisco Bay itself. The sludge could have been caught behind check dams and held until it settled from the water and only the clear liquid released. Then there would have been no destruction, no filling of the waterways, no trouble in the valley.

But adamantly the operators claimed that because they were handling a million tons at a time no check dam could be built big enough. And stoutly they maintained that their operation was necessary to the economy of the state, trumpeting that they provided hundreds of jobs, that if the legislature passed restrictive laws and they were forced to shut down, the jobs and the profits would be lost.

Barton and the valley men had heard these same arguments for years and they were not impressed. They had seen the corruption wrought on the fertile land, but the men in Sacramento had not, or did not know its meaning and listened only to the ring of gold.

And so the Night Riders waited on the mountain above the mine, waited patiently for the pressure to drop in the screaming hoses, waited for Kodyke to ride out with his men to find the cause. It was nearing midnight.

Barton, Ayres, and the two with them squatted silently on the rocky slope, ahead of the horses they had concealed in the brush. Barton had no fear of detection, guessing that it would not occur to the proud Kodyke that anyone would dare strike at the mine itself.

They felt the earth tremor of the distant explosion although they could not hear above the constant tumult below them. And they waited.

Still the water from the reservoir poured down into the flumes, nearly a thousand feet to feed the monitors. It was this drop which gave it the "head," the terrific pressure that could tear the mountain apart. Barton was beginning to wonder if he had been mistaken, if he had only imagined feeling the shock of the blast, if for some reason the main ditch had not been blown at all.

Then suddenly there was a lessening of the roar and they rose quickly to peer downward.

Water was still coming from the nozzles, but in dwindling arcs, and as they watched in the light of the working flares the streams died to a trickle. Men were running, milling like ants disturbed, and their shouts rose faintly out of the unaccustomed quiet which now filled the pit. Figures scrambled up the steep slope to the middle reservoir where the water was divided into the individual hoses, calling back that it was dry, that nothing was coming in from above.

There was a conference before the main office building. The light there was not so good as in the deep pit and Barton could not distinguish the men. Then one whom he judged to be Kodyke turned and ran toward the barns and corral. He schooled himself to patience and continued to watch.

Fifteen minutes later Kodyke, followed by some twenty mounted men and a hundred laborers on foot wound slowly up the mountain, passing the place where Barton's group lay concealed and continuing on to repair the break. They paused at the upper reservoir, talking and pointing, and then began to follow the ditch as it led out and up across the hills eastward.

Barton stood up then, slowly, straightening his cramped muscles, and spoke to Ayres and the two men.

"I don't know what we're running into. Cap and I will go ahead. You two bring the horses down in about ten minutes."

One of the riders protested but Barton silenced him with a gesture.

"If there are so many guards that Cap and I can't handle them, four men would make no difference and we can't do what we came for. If we succeed, you'll be needed later."

He dropped down then, conscious that Cap followed closely along the twisting path.

Creighton Hague and Donald Kruger still stood before the

office door, staring at the pit where a few men who had not been taken out with the labor crew worked around the silent monitors and prepared to clean up the draining sluice. They turned finally and walked back into the office and Kruger slumped in the chair behind Hague's desk.

"Damn it, you people have a small army here, and yet you can't round up that Barton. What do you want me to do, send the state guard?"

Kruger was a handsome man of fifty who, starting at seventeen as a miner in the placer camps along the American River, had clawed himself to the top, to the control of more real estate, more mines and more legislators than anyone else in the state.

Hague stood beside the desk looking old and tired and drawn. He both honored and feared Kruger, and he knew that no matter what the outcome of the night, he would be blamed.

"You don't know, you don't understand how much the people of the valley hate us."

"I don't want to understand. If I have to come up here and run this operation myself I won't need to pay you and Kodyke. Barton's got to be found and stopped. We simply can't afford to have him and his men free in the hills, free to cut our ditches and burn the flumes whenever they take the notion."

"We're trying to patrol the property."

"Patrol." Kruger's laugh held no hint of mirth. "Patrol the ditches? You're out of your mind. You know how many hundreds of miles they cover. The whole army couldn't patrol them. The only thing is to find Barton. He has to be hiding somewhere near."

The mining king stood up as if his impatience would no longer let him sit still, and paced around the office.

"He's here."

Mitch Barton had stepped quietly through the door without either man observing him. The gun in his hand covered them loosely. A moment later Cap Ayres joined him, tight faced, a gun also in his good hand.

Kruger swung around. He was not armed, and had in fact never carried a gun. Hague had a weapon in his desk but it was too far away to reach even if he had been so inclined, and he was not inclined. The look on Barton's face was enough to have made a braver man quail.

"Get over there, against that wall." Barton motioned with his gun.

It had been many years since anyone had dared order Donald Kruger to do anything. He gaped at Barton, his heavy face gaining an ugly red, then silently he obeyed. Hague joined him and at a signal from Barton both turned and faced the wall.

Mitch went over them quickly, not too surprised that he failed to find a gun.

"Take a look in the desk, Cap."

Ayres found Hague's revolver and slipped it into his pocket. Kruger turned slowly, uninvited. From his expression it was plain that he expected to die. Barton was not surprised. Had the positions been reversed he knew that Kruger would have ordered him shot without hesitation.

"What do you want?" Kruger's voice was not quite steady.

"Two things," Barton said. "First, a written statement from you that your money rigged the courts and secured the conviction of my men. A letter to the governor naming the officers and judges who accepted your bribes, and a voluntary agreement that you will close down operations until the proper dams are built to hold back the debris."

Kruger wet his lips. "How do you know that I would keep such an agreement even if I signed it?"

Barton's smile was knife thin. "Because we're going to take you with us and keep you until it is fulfilled."

Donald Kruger had been prepared to die, but he was not prepared for ruin, and that was exactly what Barton's words meant to him. Never in his whole career had he been as overextended as he was at the moment. It was only the constant replenishment of gold from the pit outside that kept his creditors from closing in to call his loans.

Impatience had always been Kruger's controlling emotion. Since early memory he had been in a hurry, and as his wealth and power had grown, so had his impatience. He had no idea of the extent of his holdings, they were that immense, but he used them for one purpose only, to get more. The ranches, the buildings in San Francisco, the mining properties here and in Nevada were all mortgaged. Even the bank he ran in San Francisco was used to supply the voracious needs of his spreading empire. He was like a tightrope walker who, as long as he was moving held his balance on the slender wire, but would fall if he ceased to advance.

"You can't do that."

Cap Ayres stepped past Barton, bringing up his shining hook. Deftly, deliberately, he brought the razor-sharp point against Kruger's neck, above the vein. The point pressed in suggestively, not enough to break the skin but enough to prove its promise.

"We can do anything we want. We could have wrecked your whole water system. That we didn't, you can thank the man you've hounded for years."

Kruger recoiled instinctively from the point of the hook and there was sweat across his broad forehead. He did not protest further but moved to the desk, sinking into the chair with such force that it creaked beneath his weight. He drew paper and a pen from the drawer and began to write, his heavy face gray and dripping moisture onto the sheet before him.

Barton watched him. This man whom he had hated for more than ten years was collapsing before his eyes, coming apart at the seams and letting the sawdust with which he was stuffed show through as if he were a rag doll.

This was the man who had controlled California. His very name being mentioned had sent men to suicide. And here he sat quaking so that writing was difficult.

Barton knew that he should feel a deep exultation. He felt nothing of the kind, but only a quick sadness at the frailty of mankind. Kruger was not alone in his reaction to Cap's hook.

90 / THE NIGHT RIDERS

It was a gruesome tool, and a man who would face a gun or even a slashing knife would turn tail and run when Cap raised his hook in anger.

Kruger was having hard going. He blotted the paper once again, and yet a third time, and he was only halfway down the sheet.

Then there was sudden sound at the door and Barton spun to face it, his gun ready. It was one of the men he had left with the horses, saying anxiously, "They're coming back."

"Who?"

"Kodyke. They spotted us from the ridge when we went to get the horses. Come here, you can hear them."

Barton spoke tensely to Kruger. "Keep writing," he said and moved quickly to the open door. Even before he reached it he heard the beat of running hoofs above. He glanced back at the man at the desk and motioned. "Come on now. Let's get going."

Kruger apparently did not hear. Barton said sharply, "Bring him, Cap."

The saloon man moved with surprising speed. He was around the desk in an instant, jerking the seated man upright with his good hand, threatening him with the hook. Barton looked at Hague.

"Lie down on the floor and stay there. If you stick your head out of the door I'll blow it off."

He followed Cap then. One of his riders was already mounted and holding the three horses. Cap pushed his prisoner toward the nearest one and curtly ordered him into the saddle.

The pounding of hoofs on the trail was louder, nearer now, and they heard someone yelling at the workmen in the pit.

Barton raced forward and swung onto the animal behind Kruger, saying in the man's ear, "Try something and I'll gut-shoot you."

He swung the horse around, seeing that Cap and the second rider were mounted, and drove his spurs against his animal's flanks just as the first of the mine police came round the rock outcrop at the trail's mouth and spurred toward the cabins.

Barton was heading due north, in the opposite direction from that in which he wanted to go, where the trees grew down within two hundred yards of the office. If they could reach the timber and separate they had a fair chance of working upward into the higher hills.

He yelled at the others to scatter, each man for himself so that they did not present a concentrated target, and in that moment the bullet struck his horse, already staggering under its double load.

The animal went down, hurling both men to the ground. The fall knocked Kruger senseless but Barton was on his feet, running toward the trees before the horse stopped kicking.

CHAPTER THIRTEEN

MARIE BEAUCHAMP had never been much of a rider. They wound up the switchbacks of the trail past the old mine dump with Rankin in the lead, the boy next and Marie following. The horse she rode was old, sure-footed, used to the mountain trails and she thankfully obeyed Rankin's order that she give it a free rein.

The cook watched them go, standing just inside the shack door armed with a cleaver. He fully expected that Rankin would try to make an end of him before riding out, but either the thought had not entered the redhead's mind or he held the old man in such contempt that he thought his death unnecessary. He saw the three figures top the rise and disappear before he turned to the corral and saddled a horse.

Mounting was awkward because of his back, and he still remembered vividly how very hard the ground had felt on the day he had been thrown, when his back was broken.

That he was alive at all was due to Barton's father. He had always been extremely grateful to the rancher, but at the moment he almost wished that he had not survived. He would have to face Barton on his return, and admit to him that he had stood aside and watched while the boy was taken away.

The horse climbed slowly and he did not urge it. It was a full hour before he reached the top and rode over the crest to halt below the tumbled rocks which served them as lookout. He found Kid Boyd without too much difficulty. Rankin had handled the guard with little trouble, clipping him neatly with the heavy barrel of his gun and then tying him securely.

Boyd was conscious when the cook found him, and as angry as a man could be.

"He came up behind me and pointed off there." Boyd gestured toward the rows of tree-covered ridges which fell away below them. "Like a fool I turned my back on him, and the sky fell in."

The cook was sympathetic. "How do you feel?"

Boyd fingered his scalp where it had been split by the force of the blow. "Terrible. What was he up to?"

The cook told him. "They've been gone the time it took me to climb up here."

Boyd twisted his aching head. "Ride on up to meet Barton. I'm going after them."

The cook stared at him. "After Fred Rankin? Your brains must be really shook up."

"He's one man," said Boyd, "and he won't know I'm on his trail. I've got a rifle, and I'll get him before he even knows I'm around."

He stood up shakily and moved with none-too-certain steps toward his horse. The cook watched him with thoughtful eyes.

"Maybe I should go along."

Boyd stopped. "Do as I tell you. The sooner Mitch knows

what's happened the more chance he'll have of catching them if I miss."

He reached his horse and half-dragged, half-lifted himself into the saddle with the help of the horn, and waited while the cook untied the animal's tether.

"Tell Barton they'll probably head for the old Emigrant Road. I'll try and leave as much trail as I can."

Then he was gone, dropping down off the ridge. The cook did not move for long minutes, and at length turned his horse northwestward, taking the trail which Barton's men had followed toward the distant mine.

Kid Boyd rode steadily, doggedly. At the first stream he crossed, he climbed down clumsily, dropping to his knees beside the rushing water and splashing the chill stuff onto his face and his buzzing head.

Revived, he mounted again and pressed on. He was gaining on those he followed, for Rankin was handicapped by the boy and the fact that the Duchess was not used to riding.

Boyd found three places where they had paused to rest, and pushed ahead in renewed confidence, but he did not catch them until they had halted for their evening meal and camp.

The fire was small and Rankin had built it before the overhang of the canyon wall which formed a near cave below the shadow of the rocks.

A tiny stream beat its way down over the stones, hemming them in. Had Rankin chosen the place purposely for defense he could not have done better. Boyd came up the canyon carefully just after full dark, and saw the glint of the fire on the far wall before he rounded the bend. He halted, backtracked, and left his horse a quarter of a mile below the camp. Then, carrying his rifle, he went forward with extreme care to the curve, pausing to peer around it.

He saw the Duchess bending above the fire and the boy beside the creek, but he failed to pick Rankin out of the shadows. It should have warned him, the apparent absence of the man. It did not. He turned, and as he turned Rankin's voice came down from above to slap him with the shock of an icy towel.

"Don't move."

Boyd saw him then, standing on a shelf and knew that the man had been watching as he came up the canyon.

"Drop that rifle."

Instead Boyd swung the gun up. He never got its barrel past shoulder level. Rankin shot him twice, deliberately, carefully, with the dispatch of a trained butcher performing a routine task.

Both bullets caught Boyd in the face, knocking him backward with their striking force. Boyd never moved after he hit the ground.

At the fire Marie Beauchamp straightened with a sharp cry of surprise. She saw the boy turn and motioned him toward her and dragged him under the rock protection as far as possible. She felt his small body shake within her grasp, and his need for reassurance steadied her own panicked nerves.

"It's all right." She said it as calmly as she could. "It's only Rankin shooting at some animal."

They stood close together, listening, waiting. They could not know that Rankin was dragging the body to one side, that he then went on down the canyon, freeing Boyd's horse, sending it galloping away before half a dozen well-hurled stones.

It was a good half hour before he came up the trail and around the bend into the firelight. Marie looked at him questioningly, fingering the tiny gun in her pocket.

"What was it?"

"Boyd," he said. "He followed us."

"Did you . . . kill him?"

He lied. "I put one bullet in his shoulder, one above his head. He got out of here fast."

She wet her lips, wanting to believe him yet not being able to quite do so.

"We've got to get out of here." He was already beside the fire, gathering up the things. "We'll have to ride all night."

She made no protest at that. If they were riding nothing else could happen, and the shadow of Barton was looming close behind them. She rose, helping as best she could. Her shoulder inadvertantly brushed his and she felt his body stiffen. He put out one hand, took her arm and turned her so that she faced him and she saw that his eyes were glowing, like a cat's in the flickering light of the dying flames.

She caught her breath then, careful not to pull away too quickly, and after a second the grip on her arm lessened and she stepped away, calling to the boy and busying herself in getting him mounted.

They rode through the night. Fred Rankin, who had not worried about anything in his fruitless life, was now obsessed by the feeling that Mitch Barton was close on his trail.

Never before had he really feared any man, and he could not understand his awe of Barton. The man had bothered him from their first meeting. In prison Fred Rankin had enjoyed a certain position. The other convicts had feared him, had taken his orders. In a sense he had run the cell block and the exercise yard.

But Barton had refused from the beginning to be cowed or impressed by his reputation, and to his own surprise Rankin had made no effort to enforce his will as he had done on so many of the other prisoners.

The boy was half asleep, his short legs tucked into the leather straps above the metal stirrups since these could not be shortened enough to accommodate the youngster. Marie Beauchamp rode at his side, watching the weaving figure, speaking to him now and again to rouse him. She herself was terribly weary. She thought that if she ever got off the horse she would never again be able to lift herself into the saddle. It was long after daybreak that she finally called to the silent rider ahead.

"I can't go any farther."

Rankin twisted in his saddle to look at her. Then he looked ahead.

"There's some kind of a cabin up on the hill. Can you make it that far?"

She raised her eyes, seeing a glimpse of log walls among the trees. "I guess so." She urged her horse onward, riding very slowly, almost counting each step the animal took.

The boy had to be lifted down. The cabin was not much when they entered it, four walls of logs, the roof sagging and threatening to cave. Marie Beauchamp was not conscious of this, not the litter strewn floor nor the gaping windows that admitted the high-country chill. On the blanket still smelling of horse's sweat she slept, the boy curled up in a tight ball against her.

She was asleep almost as soon as she lay down, and she was not aware that Rankin stood in the doorless entry watching her for a long while in the growing light of the morning before he turned back to lead the horses deep into the timber.

After that he squatted near the trail to watch the track behind them. It was cold here and he shivered. Above them the ragged peaks still held pockets of unmelted snow. At last he decided they were not closely followed and retreated to the shack wall, unrolled his blanket and slept.

The sun had already dipped behind the pines to the west before he stirred. He sat up, hardly knowing where he was for the instant, and then as memory came he straightened quickly, looking in near panic at the empty trail below. Nothing moved there and he breathed deeply in relief and turned toward the house.

The Duchess was still asleep but the boy was sitting up on the blanket at her side and Rankin motioned to him, putting a finger against his lips to invoke silence.

When the boy came out Rankin took his arm and led him part way down the hill.

"There's a creek below the trail. Go see if there's any fish in it, and stay there until I call you."

Ralph looked at him uncertainly but it did not occur to the

boy to disobey. Rankin watched him cross the trail, then turned upward and came again into the cabin.

He stood awhile just inside the doorway, then moved across until the tips of his boot toes touched the edge of the blanket.

"Duchess."

Her eyes opened slowly, soft with sleep, and she looked up at him blankly as if she had never seen him before. Then pressing memory came, and with it dread.

"Where's Ralph?"

"I sent him down to the creek."

"You sent him?"

"I wanted to talk to you."

She sat up then, and her impulse was to pull the blanket around her, for desire was hot in Rankin's green eyes.

"Now, wait."

He reached across and put a hand against the soft darkness of her hair. "You haven't forgotten the bargain, little lady?"

She wanted to pull away from him and did not dare. She sensed that any quick movement on her part would bring on violence, yet it took all of her control to say quietly, "The bargain was to be paid when we reach the railroad safely."

"You think I'm a fool?" His lips were quirking. "When we reach the railroad what's to keep you from changing your mind?"

She said steadily, "I never went back on my word in my life. Get us safely to the junction and I'll do as I promised."

"Why wait? I'm not so bad. A lot of women have found that I can be fun."

She wanted to hit him. She wished that she dare reach into her pocket for the little belly gun, but still she did not let her emotion show in her voice.

"How do I know that once you've had your payment you won't ride away and leave us stranded here?"

He grinned. "You're too pretty to leave." He caught her shoulders then and drew her to him in a surge of sudden want and found her lips, pressing his mouth tightly over hers.

98 / THE NIGHT RIDERS

There was no response and the knowledge angered him. He pushed her away from him, fumbling at the fastenings of her dress with suddenly awkward fingers. She shoved back. His fingers locked in the collar of her dress and he tore it ruthlessly as she tried to escape.

She never knew quite how she managed, trying to run for the door, to keep her footing. Rankin reached out and caught the edge of her skirt as she passed and yanked it, and the derringer which had been in the pocket thudded to the floor between them.

It was her last hope and that hope was gone now, but she ran on, jumping through the door and racing down toward the trail as hard as she could.

Her foot struck an upthrust rock. Her ankle turned and she fell so heavily that the breath was driven entirely out of her. She lay half-paralyzed, hearing the pounding of Rankin's booted feet as he came after her.

CHAPTER FOURTEEN

Mitch Barton knew that he would never make the safety of the timber. He still had fifty yards to go, and the bullets from Kodyke's gun were kicking dust pocks around him, whining angrily when they struck rock and zinged away into the darkness.

He stopped. He turned, his own gun leveling, meaning to take as many with him as he could before he was killed. And then from the corner of his eye he saw that one of his own riders was coming back for him, heard the man shout his name and turned away, ready to swing up behind his rescuer.

He never had the chance. Just as the rider reached him a bullet smashed full into the man's face, nearly tearing the head from the shoulders and toppling him from the saddle as if he had been a tenpin.

Barton's move was entirely instinctive. He leaped, catching the frightened horse by the bridle as it tried to shy away. It danced sidewise around him, but somehow he caught the horn with his free hand, somehow his foot found the stirrup and he was up, and the horse was plunging toward the trees in huge frightened leaps.

They were in the timber. Behind them the sound of firing was dying to an occasional inquiring shot. His danger was now not from Kodyke's men but from the branches of the trees under which the racing animal was carrying him. He crouched low in the saddle, his cheek almost against the horse's neck, clutching the reins tightly as if he were a jockey coming down the stretch.

The animal ran for nearly a mile, he judged, before it checked its blind pace and he could bring it to a walk and then a halt. He sat listening, but the only thing he heard was the animal's heavy breathing.

He had no idea where Cap was or where his other rider had vanished to. Nor was there any sound of pursuit. But he knew that Kodyke would already be organizing the search, that he would not get away this time if they could prevent it.

He turned west, moving at a slow pace, letting the horse regain its spent strength. He might need that strength desperately at any unpredictable moment.

It was very dark under the trees and he trusted to the animal's instinct more than to his own eyesight to choose a path. They came out finally into a deer trail that zigzagged down the slope and into a clearing. Here in the center was a rock upthrust towering above him in a jumbled pile.

Here also was moonlight, and he skirted the clearing, keeping cautiously under the shadow of the trees until he reached the far side. Then he was again in the protection of the deep timber and riding doggedly, stubbornly, putting as many miles as he could between himself and the deadly pit.

At daylight he was on the fringe of the valley. Below him lay the ranches and farms which he was risking so much to save.

At eight he reached a foothill ranch and rode into the ill-kept yard. He knew that he was taking a long chance. The reward offered for his capture represented riches to these people, who had probably never had a hundred dollars in cash in their hardscrabble lives.

But the horse was done and there were three likely looking animals in the crude corral.

A big-eyed girl of seven or eight in a much-washed dress came to the door as if sent to see who it was. She peered at him and then vanished inside and seconds later a man appeared, carrying a shotgun.

Barton's revolver was in its holster. He had lost the rifle in the run across the mine yard. He could easily have drawn the short weapon but he left it where it was as he rode toward the doorway, calling as he came up.

"I need a horse."

The man had carried the shotgun at ready. He lowered it a trifle and then said suddenly in an amazed voice, "It's Mitch Barton," and stepped out into the open.

Behind him the doorway was filled by a faded woman and three children. The girl whom Barton had seen first was the oldest. Mitch swung easily out of the saddle. He knew that there was danger but he had already staked his chance.

"A horse. I have no money, but I'll see you're paid."

"To hell with that." The man had a narrow face beneath a brush of three-day beard. His jaws were nutcracker-thin as if he had never eaten properly in his whole life. "Take Molly, the bay. She's not much on looks but she's got a lot of heart."

Barton was already unfastening the saddle. The man handed his shotgun to his wife and came to help.

"You hungry?"

"I could eat."

"Get him something."

The woman disappeared. The children held their places,

their eyes round with excitement and curiosity. The rancher took the rope from the saddle and moved toward the corral gate. Promptly the three horses retreated to the far corner of the pole enclosure.

The man cursed them in a dull monotone which held no rancor. He stepped inside and they milled away from him. But his first cast caught the bay and he brought her out, peaceful now as if the dodging maneuver had been but a game.

When the saddle was cinched he said, "Come on into the house."

Barton hesitated. Every minute he delayed might increase the chance that Kodyke's men might get between him and the old mine hideout. But he was bone weary and weak from lack of food, and he followed his host into the single room of the cabin with its stove, its homemade table and two sagging beds.

The room was filled with the smell of coffee and frying meat, and he sat at the table fighting the temptation to cross his arms upon its surface, to lower his head and go to sleep.

The food revived him, and the mare wanted to run. He followed the trail that was little more than a track as it wound along the breast of the hills, skirting the upper valley until he turned into the canyon leading him to Doan Mountain. He had traveled less than a mile when he saw a rider coming toward him and pulled off into the timber which here grew down the canyon side.

To his vast surprise he recognized the cook. He hauled out as the old man came abreast of him and hailed him, feeling a wave of worry, and saw the lined face break up with relief.

"What are you doing here?"

The cook was telling him, his words tumbling out in his eagerness.

"I rode out toward the mine and ran into some of Kodyke's police. They stopped me but I played it dumb. I guess they figured a man as old as me should know better than to get mixed up in anything."

"You should."

102 / THE NIGHT RIDERS

"So I figured that you must have circled south."

Barton was hardly listening now. "When did they pull out?"

"Yesterday afternoon. Boyd went after them. He ain't back yet."

"Which way were they headed?"

"For the old Emigrant Road. I'd say they were trying to make the railroad, probably over in Nevada."

Barton nodded. There was no point in going to the mine now. It would be miles out of his way, and he knew a short cut that would bring him out at Scott's Meadows. He urged his horse forward and the cook swung his animal.

"I'll come with you."

"You'll go back to the mine. If Cap and the rest of the crew get there and don't find me they won't know what happened."

He did not wait to see if the cook obeyed, but spurred ahead, thankful that he had a fairly fresh mount under him. Now he rode with grim purpose, filled anew with the dull, burning hatred. His anger was not directed at Rankin, but at the Duchess and at himself.

He should have known better than to leave the gunfighter at the mine. He should have realized that Marie Beauchamp would go to work on the man as soon as his own back was turned. And Rankin could not be blamed. He had been without a woman for a long time, almost as long as Barton himself.

And this woman was attractive. She had the same warm qualities which had first attracted him to his wife. That she wrapped herself in a protective sheath of self-interest as Lucy had never done did not obscure the basic appeal of her sex.

He saw the cabin long before he reached it and thought nothing of it. These hills were full of deserted shacks, remnants of the days when prospectors had quartered every foot of this rugged terrain in their wild search for gold. He was not on the trail. He had been cutting across the ridge, saving a dozen miles by the effort.

He dipped into a swale and lost sight of the rotting building, then came up the near slope through the trees and broke out

THE NIGHT RIDERS / 103

directly above the structure. He halted his horse, looking not at the cabin but studying the trail below it.

Before the advent of the railroad that trail had been a main route, over which the supplies from Sacramento had been hauled to the growing silver camp on Sun Mountain. Now that Virginia City was one of the largest towns west of the Mississippi, a railroad branch had been extended south from Reno, and the thousands of tons of freight which had once made the trail the busiest route on earth had been diverted to the iron rails. The deep wheel ruts, cut in many places to bedrock by the great wagons, were grass grown and gradually filling as storm water washed loose earth into the depressions. Nature had her own methods of marking out the ugliness left by man.

Mitch Barton had no way of knowing whether he had reached this spot ahead of or behind those he pursued, but judging by distance and time he knew that he could not be too far behind them. He sat thoughtful, resting his horse, conscious of his own weariness, relaxed and half asleep in the saddle.

And then he saw the half-naked girl rush from the cabin and run down the hillside to fall heavily before she reached the open trail.

His reflexes, usually sharp and quick-triggered, were dulled by fatigue. He watched as if seeing something unreal as Rankin dashed from the shack's doorway and loped after the fleeing figure. Not until the man had reached the half-conscious girl, had stooped to pick her up, did Barton snap awake enough to jump his horse forward.

They dropped down the steepening slope with gathering speed, the sound of the horse's hoofs deadened by the thick matting of needles beneath the tall pines.

Rankin turned, the girl limp in his arms. He saw rather than heard Barton's approach and for a moment stood frozen with surprise. Then he dropped his burden, but as he clawed for his gun the limp form rolled back against his legs and knocked him off balance.

It probably saved Barton's life, for as Rankin leaped backward to regain his footing his heel caught on the same rock over which Marie Beauchamp had tripped and he sat down hard.

Barton did not even think of the gun at his side. He threw himself from his saddle, lighting on the redhead, his fingers clawing hungrily for the throat. As he moved he knew that either he would kill the gunfighter or that Rankin would kill him. There was no such thing as quarter to Rankin's kind.

Barton's hands reached their target and closed. The force of his fall on the prone man had driven some of the wind from Rankin, but the slender, wiry body responded automatically, rolling with the litheness of a cat, wriggling and squirming to break free of the tightening grip. He succeeded, starting to rise, but Barton grabbed and caught his ankle and dumped him again, onto his face, then flung himself across the taut back and again tried to throttle the lighter man.

But Fred Rankin had spent most of his life in barroom brawls. Like a powerful worm he twisted, got onto his back and brought one knee up into Barton's groin with such paralyzing force that Mitch doubled in agony. Rankin used the instant to again break free, to come to his knees and paw for his holstered gun.

Barton kicked out in sheer desperation. His boot heel caught Rankin in the stomach and sent him staggering backward with the gun only half drawn. And then Barton struggled up and diving, caught the gun wrist as Rankin freed the weapon.

Silently they fought, body against body, Rankin lunging to bring up the gun and Barton straining to prevent it, two men made supremely strong by their need, each fighting for his life. They moved like dancers, circling in the rough trail, bending, swaying, backstepping, the muscles of their arms corded like the clutching roots of the trees around them.

Suddenly, as Barton twisted the resisting wrist, the gun exploded, and the man against him straightened convulsively and sank, turning, to crumple on the ground.

THE NIGHT RIDERS / 105

Mitch Barton stepped back raggedly, caught his balance and felt a quick lightness as he found no force against him. He felt that he was moving in a foggy dream, that none of the action of the past few minutes had actually taken place. When it was over it was over. He sat down on the upthrust stone, staring at Rankin and half expecting him to stir, to sit up. Then he heard a high yell from the trail below him and spun to see his son leaning forward, running up the grade.

Relief at seeing the boy unhurt and alive swept over him, but he called sharply, ordering Ralph to go back down to the creek, to wait there until he came.

The small figure stopped, hesitated, then obediently turned again down the hill. Barton took a deep, steadying breath in an effort to clear his head. Then he bent above the Duchess.

Her clothes were tatters. The waist she wore hung in threads from her shoulders and one white breast showed through the split in the shift. But he could find no mark upon her save the bruise above her temple where she had struck her head in falling. He kneeled and lifted her in his arms, rose heavily and began to plod upward toward the sagging cabin. He had covered less than half the distance when her eyes opened abruptly and he found himself staring down into their dark depths.

At first her face went flat with fear, then as she saw that it was Mitch Barton rather than Fred Rankin who carried her, the fear was replaced by surprise. And finally Marie Beauchamp did something she had done but seldom in her life. She began quietly to cry.

The tears were from exhaustion and relief, and a sudden sense of safety which she had never before experienced. No matter how much she hated Barton she had never feared him physically, and she had been terribly afraid as she raced down the hill away from Rankin. It had been something new to her, a terror for the boy and for herself, for she had realized that once the man had satisfied himself he would surely have killed both Ralph and her.

Mitch Barton continued to look down, watching the soundless weeping, the clear tears that squeezed from beneath her curling lashes. It was as if a gate opened, as if the wall with which this girl had so desperately shielded herself had been breached, and he was seeing the real Marie Beauchamp for the first time.

Without realizing what he did he bent his head and put his lips against hers and was startled by the quick, unthinking response, the instinctive warmth, by the way her arm slipped upward around his neck and the hot touch of her bare shoulder against his cheek.

CHAPTER FIFTEEN

THEY WERE HOLDING A COUNCIL of war, seated around the long table beside the cook shack, the extra men lounging in the shade of the small building and the two wind-twisted trees.

Nearly fifteen new riders had come in to swell the Night Riders in the last two weeks. The news that Barton's men had actually raided the mine headquarters had swept the valley like an exhilarating wind, and men who had been hesitating, without the conviction that the uprising could succeed, without the nerve to join the group early, had suddenly saddled their horses, kissed their wives and children and disappeared into the towering forests.

The exodus had been accelerated by the new activity of Kodyke's police, for Kodyke, smarting under the bitter words with which Kruger had lashed him, had intensified his efforts and his threats.

The weakness of a man like Kodyke was that his whole life had been geared to fear. He had held his place in each community he had stopped in because of the fear men had of his gun, and he attempted now to spread a blanket of terror across a region nearly a thousand miles square.

His campaign was carefully co-ordinated. In squads of ten his men rode the valley, stopping at each ranch to threaten the owners with complete destruction if they aided the Night Riders with so much as a drink of water.

His reasoning was logical enough, based on his belief that the women would be fearful for their children and their homes, that they would keep their men inactive. But he misjudged these women, for in most cases it was the ranch wife who urged her husband to go out and join the battle.

Yet Kodyke was too shrewd not to understand what was happening after the first few days, when his patrols circled back on some of the ranches and found the men vanished and the women blandly uncommunicative.

It was galling to him, the polite silence that greeted them everywhere. He did not quite dare to torture women, and short of that there seemed no way to discover how the males were able to find Barton's hideout when he himself had scoured the hills fruitlessly.

What he did not know was that Cap Ayres had set up half a dozen men as keys, that any volunteer was passed along from one to the next, never knowing his exact destination until he reached the last link in the underground railroad and was passed into the valley below Doan Mountain.

To Barton's conference the latest arrival had brought news, news that lengthened the faces of all those around the table. Kodyke had left the valley, had ridden to San Francisco to see Kruger and Kruger had appealed to the governor for the help of national militia troops in tracking down the rebellious people. Further, his plea was backed by the local judges and other law-enforcement officers.

"We can't fight the whole state." It was Cap Ayres. He perched on the end of the table absently polishing his hook as he talked, and he talked as if thinking aloud rather than making a speech. "We can't wait forever, Mitch. We have to strike now, before troops can come in."

108 / THE NIGHT RIDERS

For once Carl Dill agreed with Ayres. "If we're ever going to do anything we've got to move, and quick. Kodyke is out of the valley. His men are scattered, patrolling the ditches and hunting us. We can knock out the whole operation in twenty-four hours, blow every ditch and burn every flume." He produced a long roll of white paper and spread it across the table. On it he had meticulously plotted the entire system which fed water to the howling monitors, identifying each section with landmarks recognizable to any valley man.

Mitch Barton smiled to himself. While part of his delay in making a major strike had indeed been the lack of men, he had also been waiting for Dill and Ayres to come to agreement. A feud between his two lieutenants was not something he wanted when he risked his entire force. And now everything seemed ready, or as ready as it could ever be.

The group that had been talking among its members fell silent, impressed by the map. Whatever else Dill was or was not, he had the trained thoroughness of a good bookkeeper. They looked at the drawing, whose ink lines seemed like the branchings of a huge root system. Feeder lines led small mountain streams fresh from their fields of melting snow into holding ponds which in turn fed the main ditches and flumes, where the water dropped from heights above ten thousand feet into the big reservoir above the pits.

These people had known in their vague way that the system was extensive, but few had had any real conception of how vast a territory it covered.

Dill went on, his voice cold and precise. "Now, first we blow these." He indicated the dams that collected the ponds high in the mountains. "Then here"—his finger touched the points where the laterals entered the ditches—"and finally this." He stabbed at the deep reservoir that lay directly above the pit.

With a tone of real pleasure he said, "There are eight flumes. One of them is two and a half miles long. The rest are shorter, but the shortest is more than a mile. These we burn."

Cap shrugged. "Why? Wouldn't it be just as effective to blow out the supports and drop them into the canyons?"

Dill turned from the table to face him. "You tried that two years ago, and they were rebuilt in three days, using the same timbers. This time we don't want them rebuilt. We want to so cripple Kruger that the banks will foreclose on him."

There was an excited murmur through the group. Cap Ayres stood a moment longer, then nodded and walked away. He looked back once and saw Barton standing beside Dill, their heads bent over the sprawling map, and a feeling of discontentment filled him. Ayres realized that this was a form of jealousy, that he resented Dill and the fact that Barton was being influenced by the man's counsel. He climbed the hill, trying to shake off the sensation, and paused before the door of Marie Beauchamp's cabin. He had hardly spoken a dozen words to her since her return and knew that she had been consciously avoiding him.

He used his hook rather than his good hand, and the gleaming metal made a dull, reverberating sound on the old planks. He heard her voice and, lifting the latch, pushed the door inward.

She was seated at the plank table repairing a dress, and he eyed it thoughtfully as he crossed to take one of the stools. She saw the look and a dull flush came from her throat to tinge her round cheeks.

"You haven't asked me any questions."

He said carefully, "I didn't feel it was my place to ask."

She smiled crookedly. "Cap, you're quite a person. You've taken care of me for nearly ten years. You couldn't have done more if you'd been a father or a brother."

"Or a lover?"

Her color heightened. "Please, Cap, let's not get on that again."

"I didn't mean to." There was apology in his tone.

She reached across with a quick, understanding gesture and laid her warm hand over his.

"I was a fool to try to run away, a fool to trust Rankin."

He shrugged. "What happened to Rankin?"

"Barton killed him. Hasn't he told you?"

"He hasn't told anyone that I know of. He hasn't mentioned it. You weren't hurt?"

"Only a bruise where I fell and hit my head. Not hurt in the way you mean. But I would have been, and probably I'd also have been killed. That man was like an animal."

"So now you're grateful to Barton."

She picked up the torn dress. Her needle moved dartingly and he thought for a long moment that she had no intention of answering. Then she said softly, "I suppose I should be."

He leaned toward the table. "Stop fencing with me, Marie. I've watched you ever since you came back. And I've watched Mitch. Something else happened at Scott's Meadows." She didn't answer this and his voice roughened. "Don't get interested in Mitch Barton, child. That's the last thing you want to do. The man's as good as dead. He and Dill are out there planning the raid. They're going to wreck every ditch and flume and dam Kruger owns. Some of them are going to be killed and the rest will likely wind up back in the penitentiary."

"You're not riding with them?"

"I suppose I will, for I'm a fool too. A man has to stick with his own kind or he might as well not live. That is, unless you'll let me take you East."

Her eyes widened and she looked up. "A week ago you wouldn't have said that, Cap."

"A week ago I hadn't seen the new way you look at Mitch Barton. I don't know what did happen at Scott's Meadow but you're not the same person you were. I don't want you hurt."

She said deliberately, "All of us get hurt in one way or another, Cap. You can't live in this world without getting hurt. I'll have to take my chances, I guess, with the rest."

"Kind of a new way of thinking for you, isn't it?"

Her smile was self-mocking. "Circumstances alter cases it seems. I've got to stay here now, Cap. I'd never forgive myself if I left at this point. I've been so very wrong for so many, many years."

Cap Ayres shrugged. He stood up. He said very softly, "I had to know," and moved soundlessly out of the cabin.

When he came again into the sunlight he saw that the conference was breaking up. Dill was rolling his map into a tight cylinder. The men were drifting off by twos and threes, forming small conversational knots in the shadow of the bunkhouse and along the corral fence, some turning toward the creek. Barton was talking to the cook, then turning and moving up toward the mess hall. Ayres cut down at an angle to intercept him.

"Talk to you for a minute, Mitch?"

Barton said, "Sure. Come on in out of the sun," and led the way into the half-ruined building. A pack rat scurried from the corner, found a hole and disappeared. Barton crossed to his bunk, unstrapped his gun and sat down heavily, burying his dark head in his hands as if to contain his thoughts.

"Well, this is it."

Ayres said quietly, "When do we ride?"

"Tonight."

"When do we hit the mine?"

"At midnight tomorrow. It will take the boys that long to get to the upper reservoirs. We want the strikes to be made simultaneously."

"Sure you want to go through with it?"

Barton lifted his head to stare at his friend. Cap was not looking at him. Cap was staring at the hook as if he half-expected to see his reflection in the shiny surface.

"What do you mean by that?"

Ayres' voice was steady. "I thought maybe your thinking had changed after Scott's Meadow."

"What did she tell you about that?"

"Not a thing. I've been watching you though, Mitch."

"Watch me then." Barton stood up. He walked around the room heavily as if life were pressing too tightly against his big shoulders. "Nothing happened, Cap. Nothing at all. I got there in time."

"Something happened," said Ayres. "It shows in your eyes, in your voice. You hated her a long time. You don't hate her any more."

"I don't know," said Barton. "I don't know."

"I do. I know you pretty well, Mitch Barton. I know Marie even better. There hasn't been a day in years that I haven't watched her. She lived on hate. She kept herself going on hate. That hate is gone."

Barton showed him a tortured face. "How can you know?"

"I know," said Cap. "I know because I have to, for my own reasons. Don't do this to her, Mitch. She's had enough."

"Do what?"

"Ride with the men tonight. What if you're killed? What if you're sent back to prison?"

"What else can I do?"

"Get on your horse, take the boy, take Marie, head for Nevada and the East."

"And leave all these people leaderless?"

"I'll lead them," said Ayres. "The plan's all made. They won't know you're gone until it's all over. Each group will think you're with one of the other companies."

Barton shook his head. He came across to face Cap, to put a hand on each of the older man's shoulders.

"You're a good friend," he said. "You mean the best in the world, but you know it wouldn't work. I have to live with myself. I'd know that I ran out . . . and she'd know that she made me run out. It wouldn't do."

He turned away and Cap's eyes followed him, helpless bafflement on his square face.

"Have you talked to her, at all?"

Barton shook his head again. "Not since we got back to camp. What's there to say?"

"That you love her."

"I don't know that I do. I can't make up my mind. She's so terribly like my wife since she's let down the wall."

"The wall?"

"She surrounded herself with a wall. I think she didn't trust her feelings. I used to believe it was sheer selfishness, cold-blooded self-interest. It isn't that, Cap. It isn't that at all. Not when you understand her."

Ayres almost said, "I've understood her a lot longer than you have," then he checked himself. Instead he said, "Talk to her, Mitch. Don't ride out without talking to her. If something should happen to you she would never forget that you left her without the dignity of an understanding." He turned then and walked hurriedly out of the room, surprised at the way the sunlight stung his eyes. It hadn't been that dark in the old building.

CHAPTER SIXTEEN

Marie Beauchamp was surprised when the door was again pushed open and Mitch Barton stood in the entrance. He had not knocked. When the latch lifted she had assumed that it was Ralph returning from his regular fishing trip. She sat, the torn dress still on the table before her, looking at him, not speaking.

He came in slowly. She had never before seen him ill at ease, uncertain of himself, but the uncertainty showed now in his voice and in his walk.

"Cap thinks I ought to talk to you."

She found her tongue then. "Is it important, what Cap thinks?"

"It's important what you think . . . What *do* you think, Marie?"

114 / THE NIGHT RIDERS

Something of her old fire showed in her eyes. "You never cared before what I thought."

"I never really knew you before."

"Do you think you know me now?"

He shook his head slowly. "I doubt if any man ever understands a woman. No, I don't think that I know you. But I'm certain of one thing. I've been wrong in my judgment of you from the first."

It was her turn to protest. "But you weren't wrong. I was so blindly sure that I was right. I was burning with a sense of injustice at what you had done to me, at what I thought was the callous way you used my sister, and your apparent disinterest in your son."

His hard-lipped mouth quirked without humor. "There wasn't a great deal I could do about that."

"No," she said, "there wasn't much you could do, yet I thought you could have made some effort, at least to have him brought to the prison to see you."

"Would you have brought him?"

"You know I wouldn't have. Mitch, why have we always been at cross purposes? Why have we always hated each other so strongly?"

"I don't know," he said. "Cap thinks I'm in love with you."

"Are you?"

"I don't know that either. It's hard to reverse your thinking about a person all in a few days. I only know that when you were in my arms, when you started to cry, I couldn't bear to hurt you. I couldn't bear the thought of anyone hurting you."

"Is that what you came to say?"

"No. It was Cap who sent me. We are riding tonight. This is the showdown against Kruger. We either win or lose on this strike. We either blast him into utter ruin or we fail. Whichever way, there's a better than even chance that I'll be killed or captured and sent back to prison. And even if I do escape I still have the sentence hanging over me. There is nothing for you as far as I'm concerned. There never can be.

So I want you to take Ralph. Cap will get you both to the railroad. I've written a letter to a law firm in San Francisco with instructions for them to sell the ranch for what it will bring. As soon as you get East, write to them, tell them where you are and they will forward the money."

"Cap already offered to take us."

"Cap also offered to lead the Night Riders, to let me go away with you. I refused."

"And I refused to let him take us. I'm going to stay here as long as there is any chance of your coming back."

She rose and moved around the table then, and his arms opened instinctively to close about her shoulders.

Two hours later she stood in the cabin doorway watching them ride out, counting them unconsciously as they passed. Forty-three. Grim-faced, silent, taut. Their clothes were worn out, their faces bearded, but now their eyes were alive. For the first time in ten weary years each man was acting, going out to strike against the octopus which had ruined them all.

It was full dark when they topped out of the canyon. Mitch Barton halted, swinging his horse around.

"We split here," he said calmly. "Carl, take twelve men and hit the upper reservoirs. I don't care how many guards there are. Blow them up somehow."

"Cap, you take fifteen men. Your job is to burn the flumes. The rest of you come with me." He glanced at the watch he carried. "Does your time agree with me? We hit tomorrow night at midnight. You'd better split your forces. If any of Kodyke's patrols run into a large party they'll be suspicious. Go in twos and threes. Keep out of sight as much as possible. Don't start destroying the reservoirs until twelve. But don't be late."

He raised his hand for advance then, and rode out at the head of his party. When he had covered a quarter of a mile he looked back. Both Cap's and Dill's people had disappeared into the timber. He divided his own crew then into four segments,

116 / **THE NIGHT RIDERS**

telling them to rendezvous a mile above the Ione headquarters, assigning to each group a route and impressing on them that they must ride through the night, hide during the day and move on up to the pit only after the next dark.

With two men he headed along the flank of the valley, knowing that he was taking a chance, but the letter to the lawyers was heavy in his pocket.

He reached a hill ranch five miles above his own old spread and rode without hesitation into the yard. A woman and three children came to the door, the woman holding a shotgun ready for instant use over the head of the oldest child. Barton made no attempt to step down. He pulled the letter and a silver dollar from his pocket, holding up the coin so that they could see it, and calling, "I want this letter taken into the Ferry and mailed."

They watched him in uncertain silence. He took a further chance and said, "I'm Mitch Barton."

At once the woman lowered the gun. She motioned the oldest boy forward, a twelve year old.

"You don't have to pay us nothing, Mr. Barton. My man's riding with you. His name's Sparks. Art Sparks."

Barton did not know the man but he did not admit it. He said, "I'll tell him. Here, catch." He tossed the dollar through the air to the boy. "Get it in the mail this afternoon, will you, son?"

The boy nodded, impressed.

Then they were gone, riding out of the yard less than five minutes after they had entered it. But as they climbed the hill again a figure they did not see came down through the trees. This rider halted his horse to watch them cautiously, and a rising excitement welled through him.

Finley Barton was a head shorter than his cousin and four years younger. He had not seen Mitch since the latter had gone to prison, but they had been raised on the same ranch together, and he knew that his identification could not be mistaken. He was tempted to pull the gun at his belt. A lucky shot could be worth ten thousand dollars to him, besides the possibility that if something happened to Barton's son he would inherit the ranch. But Barton was followed by two men, and he could not tell whether other Night Riders were close at hand. Finley was not a bold man. He watched them pass, slumped in his saddle trying to decide how best to turn the chance discovery to his advantage.

He decided to backtrack them, guessing that they had come from the still unknown hideaway, but in the darkness of the growing night he found it impossible to follow their trail. Finally he camped without a fire and spent the night huddled in his blanket.

At first dawn he was up, working his way back through the timber patiently, noting the disturbed needles where the three horses had passed. The tracking led him to the canyon which ran up, beckoning, straight toward the barren, snowcapped slopes of Doan Mountain, and he guessed long before he came up on the shoulder that they were holed up at the old Haskell mine.

He cursed his own stupidity for not having thought of the mine and its boxed canyon long before. Yet he had not known there was still a way in, with the road washed out. He reached a ridge and dismounted, noting the number of tracks on the flinty soil, feeling his pulse race.

Had there been a lookout Finley Barton would have been discovered long before he reached that point, but since he meant to strike and scatter his men that night, Barton had not felt it necessary to leave anyone except the cook.

Finley stood peering down at the old buildings, seeing the tiny plume of smoke rising listlessly from the rusty stovepipe of the cook shack. Then he hurried back to his horse, mounted and rode with careless haste for Morgan's Ferry.

Along with the rest of the valley Finley knew that Kodyke had gone to San Francisco, but he was aware of something the rest did not know, that the head of the mine police was due to return that morning.

He was sitting on the steps of the stage station when the mudwagon pulled in, the open body swaying and creaking on the leather braces. Kodyke was first out of the coach. He saw Finley on the steps and ignored him. Their agreement was that they should never speak in public, but Finley was in too much of a hurry to wait to catch Kodyke alone. He rose, falling into step with the gunman, and his voice trembled with excitement.

"I've found Mitch's hideout."

Kodyke stopped. He turned slowly, his odd eyes looking more dead than usual. For three days he had been the target of abuse from Kruger and the mining king's associates and he had come back grimly resolved that he would kill Mitchell Barton if he had to quarter every foot of the mountain country himself. He asked one word: "Where?"

"The old Haskell mine on Doan Mountain."

"How far away is it?"

"Twenty miles if you take the short cut. Sixty by the regular trail."

"Can you get through the short cut?"

"I can."

"How many men with Barton?"

"I don't know."

Kodyke nodded. He moved on down the street to the hotel. Three of his police were on the porch there. They stood up as he mounted the steps.

"How many of you in town?" Kodyke asked brusquely.

"Twelve," the tallest man said.

"Get your horses."

In half an hour the small band rode out of town. Kodyke was in the lead with Finley Barton at his side. Kodyke looked at his companion curiously. He had never had any illusions about his fellow men, nor did he usually set in judgment on their actions. But he failed to understand Finley's motives, and therefore distrusted them.

Finley Barton was a small man, with the resentment against

the world often held by those of short stature. This much Kodyke recognized. The resentment included the older cousin, and this too Kodyke knew, but it still did not completely explain Finley's willingness, no, eagerness to betray the man on whose ranch he lived, the man who had raised him from childhood.

The ranch could be the key. It was not as badly affected by the silt as some of the lower valley places were, but parts of it were blighted and it seemed odd that Finley should side with the very interests who were destroying the land on which he lived. He put his thoughts into careful words.

"You hate your cousin, don't you?"

Finley had been so deeply immersed in his own thoughts that he had not sensed that the other was studying him. He came to with a start and glanced inquiringly at the gunman.

"We never liked each other." His voice was short.

"I suppose that if he wins his play he'll kick you off the property."

"Probably." Finley sounded almost indifferent.

"And if we kill him or send him back to jail, what then?"

Finley turned his head. "I don't know. I suppose I'll have the court appoint me the boy's guardian and go on running the ranch for him."

"The Yankee Duchess will fight you there."

Finley Barton showed his first spark of feeling. "Fight *me* . . . I'll fight *her*. I'll show that woman that she can't step out of her place. I'll break her if it's the last thing I do."

Kodyke smiled inside. He had his answer. It was the girl who was the key to the situation, to Finley's attitude. He said, "She'll be at the hideout," and watched the lines around Finley's mouth harden.

"I know."

Kodyke said nothing further, but he had no intention of letting Finley have his way with the girl. He had his own plans for her.

THE NIGHT RIDERS

The trail narrowed until it was little more than a deer path, the country roughened and the rolling, thin-soiled foothills gave way to the higher peaks. The scrub oak, dotting the small grassy parks dropped behind and rock bursts, left by ancient volcanic explosions, lifted about them like silent monuments. There was a grandeur, an emptiness to this land which always affected Kodyke. Fundamentally a man of the towns, he was more at home at a saloon poker table than in the vastness of the towering hills.

Ahead of them rose a sheer rock wall, a good thousand feet into the deep blue of the sunlit sky. The path seemed to lead abruptly to the wall and Kodyke glanced speculatively at the canyon sides flanking them to right and left, wondering if Finley were wrong, if there was a way a man could follow up that shining face.

He was not long in learning, for within minutes the track turned up and wound along a fault so narrow in places that Kodyke's knees brushed the rough stone on his right.

At Finley's suggestion he gave the horse its head, letting the animal pick its footing slowly, with an instinct far surer than man's. Behind him he heard the muttered curses of his crew.

These men had ridden the back trails for most of their case-hardened lives, but none of them liked danger and there was danger here, for a misstep by a frightened horse could plunge them to the bottom of the box canyon below. And there were many things that could frighten a horse, a buzzing snake disturbed from its lurking place in a rock crevass by their approach, a falling stone rolling down from above, a blowing bush clinging to an inch of soil in a slender fissure.

Somehow they topped out without accident and reined in to rest the horses and let their own nerves uncoil. Kodyke's cigarette was without taste against the salty feeling in his mouth as he looked back along the way they had come.

"How'd you ever find that trace?"

"Mitch found it. Mitch used to roam these hills when we were kids. He made me come with him. I'll never forget the first time we climbed this way. We did it on foot, and then when Mitch had assured himself it could be done, he made me go back down and bring up the animals."

Kodyke motioned to his men and urged his horse forward again, crossing a high mountain meadow which was bordered to the east by the reaching slopes of Doan Mountain.

"How much farther?"

Finley shrugged. "Maybe five or six miles. The old road circled the mountain and went up on the south, but it was washed out long ago. We have to go over the shoulder and drop down in. It's a tough trail."

"As bad as the one we just came up?"

"No, it's safe enough, but it twists back and forth on itself like a ladder."

"And you're sure there wasn't a lookout?"

"I didn't see any."

"Come on."

Ralph Barton saw them first. He was climbing up from the creek with a string of fair-sized trout and happened to glance up at the trail as the long column wound its way downward. He began to run toward his aunt's cabin, shouting.

"They're back. They're coming back."

It didn't occur to him that these were strangers, were enemies. He had lived in this valley unmolested for weeks.

The cook heard his yell. The cook stepped from the bunkhouse and shaded his eyes with his hand. A shot was his first warning that these were not Barton's men. The bullet struck the old wall close to his head and he ducked back inside, grabbing a shotgun from its place above the stove and ramming two brass cartridges into the barrel.

The boy had almost reached the cabin when the shot came. The Duchess had the door already open, and caught his small shoulder and hauled him inside. He had dropped the string of fish and would have gone back for them, but she shoved him into the corner, ordering him to crawl under the bunk. For

122 / THE NIGHT RIDERS

herself she got the little derringer and slipped it into her apron pocket.

Then she moved to the window in time to see Kodyke and Finley Barton drop off the side of the swelling dump, their men fanning out behind them as they reached the more level ground so that they rode forward carefully in a watchful skirmish line.

Kodyke had already guessed that Barton and the majority of his crew were absent, and the knowledge drove him with impatience as he visualized what they might be doing to the mines. But now that he had come this far he meant to wipe out the place and any men who remained.

The cook still stood just inside the bunkhouse door, and the broken hands which held the twin-barreled shotgun shook as he raised it. But he meant to protect the girl and the boy if he possibly could. Yet at the last minute, before he pulled the trigger his nerve failed. What good would his shot do? It might get that toad Finley, or even Kodyke, but the rest of the riders would then drag him out and kill him.

Kodyke had seen him above as he ducked into the building. He pulled up his horse a hundred yards short of the structure and sent his call across the silent space.

"Come out of there, all of you."

The cook knew that they thought there were others in the bunkhouse. He dropped the gun and stepped through the door, his hands raised shoulder-high, blinking as he came into the sunlight.

Kodyke watched him with the intentness of a cobra. "How many more in there?"

"None." The cook kept his voice steady with a conscious effort.

"Take a look, Morton."

One of the riders put his horse forward, holding his gun ready. He did not dismount but rode up to the door and peered inside.

"Guess he's right."

Reassured, Kodyke advanced to where the cook was standing.

"Where's Barton?"

"Never heard of him."

Kodyke drew his gun in a single, leisurely sweep. The cook's eyes widened with panic, but the expected bullet did not come. Instead Kodyke lashed suddenly with the gun barrel against the side of the aged head. Purposely the blow was not solid. He did not put the cook out, but knocked him from his feet so that he hit the ground hard and lay half-stunned where he fell.

Kodyke looked down on him in cold anger. "Listen to me, old man. I have no time to play games. If you don't tell me what I want to know I'll break your fingers, one at a time. Then your arms and finally your legs.

"Where is Barton?"

"They rode out."

"For the mines?"

"I guess so."

"On your feet."

The cook dragged himself up slowly, painfully. Kodyke turned savagely on Finley. "Why didn't you tell me Barton wasn't here?"

The man refused to meet the other's eyes. "I thought he'd be back."

"You thought . . . then you knew he wasn't here."

Hesitantly Finley told of seeing Barton and the two riders, of backtracking them.

"Why didn't you tell me this before? We've wasted half a day."

He would have gone on belaboring Finley but Marie Beauchamp was now running from her cabin. She pushed between Kodyke and the cook.

"Leave him alone."

At the sight of her Finley Barton made a noise deep in his throat. He swung down, grabbing and jerking her arm.

"Get out of the way, you bitch. This is one time you won't interfere. You haven't got Cap Ayres and that damned hook here now."

Kodyke dropped from his horse, his gun swinging up in the same motion, and the barrel cracked sharply against the side of Finley's head and knocked him to the ground. The mine policeman stood over the fallen figure, raging.

"If you ever put your hands on her again I'll kill you."

He turned then and took off his hat, and there was courtliness in his manner as he told her, "My fight isn't with you, ma'am, remember that. If you need anything, call on Alf Kodyke."

Kodyke did not wait for her reply but swung again, stirring the prostrate Finley with his toe. "Take her and the boy to the ranch. And if you so much as say one word out of line to her I'll see you hang." He glanced at his men. "Come on. Let's ride."

CHAPTER SEVENTEEN

THE THUNDER OF THE MONITORS encompassed the night, shaking the earth with their all-destroying force. Barton and his men, waiting in the timber, felt the constant, overwhelming blasting sound as if it were directed against them trying to blow them from the mountain. The men were nervous, checking their guns, waiting impatiently for the signal.

Barton looked at his watch. It was still early, not quite eleven o'clock. He said tensely:

"I'm going down there and have a look. I want to know how many men are around the headquarters before we strike. Don't move until I come back, unless I don't get back by twelve. If I don't you'll know something's happened. In that case, Gillis, you're in charge. Use half the men to hit the pits, the others to blow the reservoir above us. I want every hose slashed. I want the crew rounded up and held in the bunkhouse."

He could not see their faces clearly in the dim light from the moon which filtered through the trees, but he could sense their uneasiness. He started down the hill then, working through the brush, feeling the needles soft yet slick beneath his boot soles.

Creighton Hague was alone in the mine office, the desk before him stacked with shipping slips. In the safe at his right was over a hundred thousand dollars in new gold, waiting only Kodyke's return to be forwarded to the San Francisco mint. He sighed, rose, and started over to close the safe door.

From his position outside the window Mitch Barton saw the gold and guessed the man's next step. He had had no intention of showing himself at this time, but now he did not want that safe door closed and locked. He drew his gun and moved like a shadow, sideways to the entrance. Hague had just bent before the safe when Barton came in behind him.

Hague froze in his position. Always in a mine manager's mind was the possibility of holdup, and it did not occur to him for the instant that it could be Barton again. At his side dangled a cord which connected to a wire running across the trampled ground and into the police building. A pull on that cord would ring the gong in Kodyke's office. His hand strayed toward it, but Barton's voice was tense.

"One move and I'll shoot you."

Hague turned then. He recognized Barton and his face went white beneath the even layer of his tan. His lips were stiff and his articulation difficult.

"Where'd you come from?"

Barton grinned wolfishly. "We're all around you, Hague. This is the end of it." He glanced at the two canvas bags lying in the corner. "Put that gold into those sacks, quickly."

Protest jumped to Hague's lips. There was a gun again in the desk drawer and the alarm tantalizingly out of reach.

126 / THE NIGHT RIDERS

Kodyke wasn't here, and most of the mine police had either ridden to the Ferry to meet their chief or were out patrolling the upper reservoirs and ditches; but there were still half a dozen at the barracks and nearly a hundred workmen at the pit. He said in a voice which he strove to make calm, "Why don't you just go on away from here while you can?"

Barton said, "You just put the gold in the sacks." His gun jerked suggestively, and Hague turned slowly to pick up the bags.

Barton watched him with eyes which seemed to glow a little. Hague carried the sacks to the safe, transferring to them the small gold bars. These were not regulation bars, but had been cast in molds only a quarter of the normal size to facilitate handling.

Barton had no idea how much was in the safe but he judged that each sack would weigh thirty or forty pounds. He smiled as Hague finished filling them and tied the mouths with wire, unable to keep back one outburst.

"This is outright robbery!"

Barton hit him then. The gun's barrel made a dull crunching sound as it struck the side of the man's head, and Creighton Hague dropped soundlessly. For a moment Barton stood over him, glancing around for something with which to tie him, then noise outside made him catch up the sacks in the crook of his arm. They were heavier than he had anticipated. They weighed more nearly eighty to a hundred pounds. He swung to the doorway and had almost reached it when a man loomed suddenly there. Barton had never seen him before, nor had the man seen Barton, but he saw the sacks, saw the drawn gun in Barton's hand and saw Hague's sprawled figure before the open safe. His startled yell split the night.

Barton's shot, striking the man fully, was all the alarm needed. Mitch ran for the door, across the fallen form and outside. Here it was half-light from the unobstructed moon and the reflected glow of the working torches in the pit. In this eerie light he saw men boiling from the police barracks.

He turned, intending to run north toward the woods as he had before, but workers tumbling from the big bunkhouse rushed out to cut his path. He spun again, cornered as the first spate of shots sent bullets kicking dirt around his feet.

He ran for the pit. He had no choice. They were converging on him from two angles. A bullet came out of the darkness to strike one of the sacks cradled in his left arm, knocking it from his grasp before singing off into the night. He ran on, letting the second sack slowly slide away.

Before him in a half-crescent twenty-five monitors still sent their streams lancing against the face of the four-hundred-foot-thick strain of gravel. None of the operators who stood directing the giant nozzles could hear the shots behind them, so deafened were they by the continual roar. Barton charged toward the center nozzle. He was on the operator before the man was even conscious of his presence. His gun rose and fell. The man dropped. Barton seized the lever which controlled the pivot on which the nozzle swiveled and swung it around in a ninety-degree turn. The terrible water became a scythe, knocking the workmen on his right from their platforms, sending them sprawling like tenpins. He swung on, bringing the stream to play on the group chasing him. It was as if a whirlwind mowed them down, cutting their legs from under them and battering them to the uneven floor of the pit.

There was not one man on that side still standing, but suddenly the operator working on Barton's left happened to turn his head, to see in amazement what Barton was doing. For an instant he sat frozen where he was, then as comprehension came he threw his own nozzle in Barton's direction. Had he depressed his monitor he would have knocked Mitch out of the fight on the instant, but the stream was aimed too high. It formed an arcing cascade twenty feet above Barton's head, warning him, and at once Barton whirled his giant weapon to pound at his new attacker. The water struck its target, driving him in a flying fall twenty feet before it dumped him hard against the muddy ground.

128 / THE NIGHT RIDERS

The operators lined beyond him caught some hint of the action and began to turn. Barton's stream beat down the closest four but failed to reach the fifth.

By a like token that man could not reach Barton, and they sat for precious minutes fighting the strange and futile duel, straining against their machines as if their wills alone could force the water to jet the extra distance.

Still the awesome streams fell innocently in gushing spray like the fountains of Paris gone mad.

And then across the roar the night above them exploded with a violence which even dulled the monitors. The dam which held the reservoir rose in a volcano of earth and water, and within seconds the serpentine hoses began to flatten, the pile-driving streams lowered and died to harmless sprays then shrank to trickles.

The cessation of sound was more startling than the blast which preceded it. It was as if someone had hurled a deadening blanket over the entire area.

Barton stood rigid, his hands still locked on the control, staring around at the scattered, stunned men. Then he came alive and knew that if he were to escape he must do so before they regained their own senses.

He was running now, back toward the mine buildings, trying to retrace his steps. He found one of the fallen sacks but not the second, and he had no time to search. Half of the torches had been driven out by the swinging swaths of water but the others burned brightly, their whale-oil flames sending up a pillar of brilliance into the now silent night.

He reached the corner of the main building and rounded it, intending to race for the trees where he had left his men, but in that moment Creighton Hague stumbled from the doorway, a gun in his fist. Barton stopped. He was breathless, hampered by the sack of gold he carried, his own gun jammed in his wet holster.

Hague's first shot took his hat. The second tore through his pants without breaking the skin of his leg. And then his gun was free and he was remembering something his father had told him a long time before: *"Don't hurry. It is better to have one shot and make it tell than to empty your gun without aiming well."*

He fired coolly, deliberately. He saw the bullet strike Hague's face and saw the man disappear as he was hurled back into the dark office. Then he was running again, for the timber. Before he reached it his men broke from it, coming toward him, and he slowed.

They met and escorted him to the edge of the trees, standing there to look out at the havoc wrought by the fight with the monitors. Barton passed the sack to the nearest man.

"There's another like it back there somewhere. I'm going after it."

Gillis caught his arm. "Don't be a fool. There must be thirty or forty men out there. Maybe more."

He broke off suddenly, tensing. They all heard it, the steady pound of horses on the lower trail. They looked at each other and then without words dived into the shelter of the trees.

Kodyke had been three miles away when the blast shook him and the howl of the monitors died. He swore sharply, urging his trail-weary horse forward, motioning to his followers, and they spurred for the mine.

They broke out of the timber to see the knot of people gathered at the edge of the pit, and raced to them, Kodyke yelling as he came.

"What happened?"

A dozen voices answered at once. Out of the babble of their words he got a quick, graphic picture and swung away, hurrying to the office building, wondering where Hague was and cursing him as he dropped from his saddle and ran for the office door.

The first thing he saw inside was Creighton Hague, spread on his back, his face a bloody mass, unrecognizable. Kodyke only glanced at him. He had no further interest in Hague for the empty, gaping safe had caught his eye. He stared at it for

130 / **THE NIGHT RIDERS**

a long moment, then flung out of the office and back to his saddle.

The men from the pit were gathering about him, mingling with the riders who had come in with him. He glared at them without seeing them, and then raised his head to the dark trees above and sent his voice ringing through the silence.

"Barton, can you hear me?"

There was a long moment of quiet, then Barton's voice reached him faintly.

"I hear you."

Kodyke called, "I just thought you'd like to know that I have your son and the Duchess. I sent them to the ranch with your cousin."

Barton had been squatting beside a rock, watching the play around the office. He rose as if straightened by an uncoiling spring, then stood with not a muscle moving. When he called in return he hardly recognized his own voice.

"I don't believe you. Where would you get them?"

"At a place called the Haskell mine. If you think I'm lying, the trail zigzags down beside the old dump. Ride back there and you'll find that we burned every building to the ground."

Barton breathed deeply before he answered again. "All right. What do you want?"

"Give yourself up. Return the two gold sacks you stole. Disperse your men."

"You're too late," said Barton. "At the same time we blew this reservoir we blew the main one. Even now we are cutting your ditches and burning your flumes. By morning there won't be a hundred feet of ditch in your whole system that will hold water. It will take months, years to rebuild. Donald Kruger is through."

He turned away then, exhausted, motioning his group to mount, hearing one of them say in disappointment, "Aren't we going to stay and wipe them out?"

"Why?" Barton looked at him. "It's finished."

Gillis asked softly, "What about your boy?"

"What about him?" Barton's voice was weary. "They won't kill him. They can't use him to prevent my wrecking their operation because that's already done. It's all finished."

He moved to his horse. He climbed heavily to the saddle. The bag of gold he gave to Gillis.

"Get this out of the country. Whatever money you can raise on it send back to Cap Ayres in the valley. Let him take care of the people who need it most."

Gillis looked at him, startled. "What are you going to do?"

Barton lifted his shoulders. "Get my son. Then I'm going to try to get out of the country."

He rode away alone, into the night.

Below them Kodyke's men were still clustered about their leader as he gave rapid orders.

"Track back along the ditches. You, Jonas, ride for San Francisco. Take relays. A hundred dollars if you make it in twelve hours. Get word to Kruger, tell him what's happened. He's got to know before anyone else does. He'll have to cover himself as best he can."

Jonas hesitated. "Wouldn't it be better if you went yourself?"

Kodyke shook his head. "I've got business here, at the Barton ranch." He swung to his saddle. "Tell Kruger I'll see him in a few days."

CHAPTER EIGHTEEN

At two o'clock the following afternoon Jonas turned his tired animal through the gates of Donald Kruger's rolling Burlingame estate and rode toward the forty-room mansion which Kruger had built for himself in the exact center of the six-hundred-acre block.

Some twenty weekend guests milled about the spacious

lawns, turning in surprise as the dusty rider put his horse directly across the turf toward where the host was playing croquet with three women.

Kruger looked up, annoyed, failing to recognize Jonas as one of the mine police. He strode forward angrily, carrying the mallet as he would a weapon.

"Here now. What do you want?"

Jonas wiped his dry mouth with the back of his grimy hand. He was riding the seventh horse, and two of them had dropped after he pulled off the saddle. It was exactly eleven hours and twenty minutes since he had left Ione.

"Message from Kodyke."

At once Kruger was alert, the anger vanishing from his voice. "What is it?"

"Maybe we'd better be alone when I tell you."

A wave of apprehension swept over the mine owner.

"Come into the house then."

He turned to lead the way. Jonas stepped from his mount before the wide marble steps. A groom came running to take the lines, and Jonas followed Kruger through the arching hall and into the great mahogany-paneled study. There was a decanter of brandy on the side table and the rider's eyes lighted.

"I could use a drink."

Silently Kruger poured, and shuddered as the man swallowed the glass full at a single draught, with no more respect than if the precious liquor were Pennsylvania whiskey.

"Kodyke said you'd give me a hundred dollars if I made it here in less than twelve hours. I did."

Impatiently Kruger produced the money and laid it on the table between them.

"Now will you tell me what's happened?"

Jonas told the story in short, curt sentences. When he finished Kruger slumped into the armchair behind the desk, the ruddiness drained from his face.

"Are you sure they blew the upper reservoir and burned the flumes?"

THE NIGHT RIDERS / 133

Jonas shook his head. "I'm not sure of anything. Kodyke just said to get the word to you so you could protect yourself before the news leaks out."

Kruger was thinking aloud. "How soon will that be?"

Jonas shrugged. "Depends on when somebody from the mine goes down to the Ferry. I imagine Kodyke will see they don't go too soon. And Barton's people aren't likely to talk, not right away. None of them will want to allow they had a hand in it."

Kruger pulled out another hundred dollars. "Get back to the mine as fast as you can. Tell Kodyke to keep me informed but to try to keep everybody else from talking." Without waiting for the man's reply he hurried into the hall, calling for the groom to bring around the fastest team.

Two hours later Donald Kruger walked into the lobby of the Central Pacific Bank, noting the surprise of the employees as he moved quickly back to his own office. He sent runners at once to half a dozen of his associates, and the meeting which was held in the bank's board room changed the course of the financial history of California.

Within six hours Kruger had disposed of over a hundred pieces of San Francisco real estate. He had sold two ranches in Los Angeles county and one in Santa Barbara.

When the market opened the following morning his agents were busy on the floor of the Exchange selling stock, not only in the hydraulic mine but also in his Comstock holdings. In a desperate attempt to cover his commitments Donald Kruger was attempting to raise fifty million dollars.

By evening of the second day he was within ten million of his goal, but in doing it he had depressed the value of mining stocks on the Exchange by at least one third.

One thing remained, the assets of his own bank, and within twenty-four hours he had stolen two thirds of its cash reserve. Then, hopeful that with a little more time he could weather the crisis, he started for Sacramento.

Word of the events in the valley and hills had finally reached

134 / THE NIGHT RIDERS

the Bay area. As he rode the steam cars up the river he glowered at the black type which blazoned the news of Barton's raid on the mining property.

In the governor's office, supported by three of the most powerful state senators, he made his bold plea for rescue of his toppling empire.

"This is nothing but anarchy." He was pacing viciously back and forth across the office of the new gubernatorial mansion. "Law and order have completely broken down in the valley. My private sources tell me that two judges have been threatened, that the sheriff at Morgan's Ferry has resigned, that the Night Riders are in full control. There is only one solution, Your Excellency, to order out the State Guard."

The first contingent of State Guard marched into Morgan's Ferry on the afternoon of the fourteenth and set up their tents along the river. And on orders the captain in charge reported to Alf Kodyke.

Kodyke had taken over Cap Ayres' abandoned Oriental Saloon as his headquarters, and here he held his court. The captain, in civilian life the owner of a bakery, showed marked distaste for the role assigned him, but Kodyke overrode him.

"You are here to take my orders," he said coldly. "And those orders come directly from Sacramento."

The captain shrugged. "What is it you want me to do?"

"Keep peace here. Patrol the lower valley. I need my men at Ione and higher. We have a thousand laborers coming in to rebuild the flumes."

The captain stiffened. "We're not working for the mining company, Mr. Kodyke. We are here to preserve order, and personally I've seen no sign of disorder. I am so reporting to Sacramento."

Kodyke's voice deepened with his feeling. "You've seen no disorder because my men are alert. Believe me, if we weren't here standing guard the whole valley would be a battleground. There are still desperate men in the hills, escaped convicts whom we have not yet caught. That's another reason why I want you here, to free me to capture them."

He watched the captain go, then stood up slowly. He was obsessed by a sense of failure. Kruger had given him the task of catching Mitch Barton and he had not done so. He would feel certain that Barton and the few men remaining with him had already slipped out of the country but for one thing, the boy.

Barton's son was still at the ranch, and so was the Duchess, bait for a painstakingly laid mantrap. Every road, every trail leading to the old Barton property was watched day and night, and his men had orders to let anyone ride in but to make sure no one escaped.

Mitch Barton was fully aware of the trap. High in the hills in a small meadow close to the headwaters of the Feather River he and Cap Ayres and Carl Dill had made a well-hidden camp. The two had followed the leader away from the scene at Ione, and his protests had not made them turn back. The little group was all that remained of the rebellious forty who had ridden through the night to destroy the wide-flung mining system.

There was hostility in the camp, mistrust and misunderstanding still alive between Ayres and Dill. Mitch Barton knew it and watched them across the tiny fire that had cooked their breakfast and was assailed by a sense of failure as keen as Kodyke's.

Ayres was grumbling. "You were so certain that Kruger would collapse, that if we stopped the flow of gold from the mine he would fold immediately. If you ask me, the reports sound like he's stronger than ever."

Carl Dill was mending the girth of his saddle. He looked up, hot temper in his eyes, and his bearded jaw set grimly.

"He is ruined. He's got to be."

"Sure," Ayres laughed sourly. "He's ruined fine. Kodyke rules the valley as if he had a deed to it. The government is sending in troops. Gillis says they're due in the Ferry today.

The flumes will be rebuilt, the ranchers who rode with us have been driven out. You played hell, you did. The country was bad off before, but it's a thousand times worse now."

The words were directed at Dill but they bit deep into Barton.

"You think it would have been better if I'd stayed in prison?" he said quietly.

Cap looked at him. He had no real desire to quarrel with Barton, yet he had a savage urge to hurt someone, almost anyone, to relieve the inner tension which gripped him.

"If you want the truth, yes. Who have you helped? What have you accomplished? The valley is more desperate than it's ever been."

"I know it."

"And look at Marie, she and your son are prisoners. God knows what's happening to them."

"Stop it." Barton had had enough. "I'm going down there now."

At once Cap was sorry for his outburst. "Don't be a fool, Mitch. Don't pay any attention to me. Gillis says the ranch is guarded more tightly than the mine."

"I'll get through."

"And what good will that do?"

Barton did not answer but rose and moved out toward where the hobbled horses were grazing.

Cap sighed. "I've done it now." He was speaking more to himself than to Dill. "We'd better ride with him."

"For what?" Dill made no move to follow.

Cap turned to stare at him and did not hide the contempt he felt. "You started this. You planned it, and your only reason was revenge."

The ex-auditor shrugged and his hand shifted a little toward the butt of the gun slung at his hip.

Cap half-raised his hook. "Don't try it. You're a thief and a liar and you set all this up. Ride out. If I ever see you again I'll kill you."

He turned his back as if daring Dill to shoot, and stalked after Mitch Barton. Dill stood rigid, watching, his tongue circling his dry lips. He had never been a man given to deep physical violence and his impulse to challenge Ayres frightened him. He waited until they rode down the twisting path, out of the meadow, then driven by some inner devil of his own he hurriedly saddled his horse and swung up.

He did not follow the others. He was headed this time for San Francisco as fast as he could get there, cursing himself as he rode. He should have realized before that by fighting Kruger in the valley he was using weapons he did not understand. Somehow Kruger had managed to ride out the closing of the mines. It was up to him, Dill, to find out how, to strike the man in whatever was now his weakest spot.

He rode tensely, doggedly. He bought a horse at a mountain ranch. He bought another in a tiny town beside the river. Darkness came but he did not stop. To the south waited the city, and somewhere in the snarl of its financial dealings lay the answer he sought.

CHAPTER NINETEEN

MITCH BARTON GAVE NO SIGN that he knew Cap Ayres was with him. He rode steadily yet without apparent hurry, like a man setting off on a long journey.

Cap made no effort to break the silence. He trailed perhaps a dozen yards behind his friend, accommodating the speed of his horse to the one in front.

They camped that night in the lower canyon, careful of their fire, knowing that these hills were being scoured by Kodyke's vengeful men, and it was not until they had wolfed the scanty meal that Barton looked fully at Ayres.

"Say it."

"Say what?" Cap was taken aback by the suddenness of the words.

"That I'm a fool. That the ranch is a baited trap and that I'm riding into it just as they hope."

Cap found his stubby pipe and began packing the bowl with care. "I don't know what else you could do."

Barton's mouth twisted. "Meaning?"

"If you didn't go, I'd go anyhow. I wouldn't leave Marie with Finley, let alone Kodyke."

Barton came to his feet.

"Where you think you're going?" Cap asked.

"I can't sleep now."

Cap sighed. He wished that he was as young a man as Barton. He almost wished he had not spoken. He said soberly, "I hope you have a plan."

"I think I do."

Barton did not elaborate as he mounted and again turned downcanyon. He rode with care despite his apparent haste. Three times during the night they heard riders approach and pulled off the trail into the dark trees, letting them pass without learning who they were.

At daylight Barton turned up a side canyon, found shade beneath a clump of oak trees, hid the horses around the bend, and with Cap stretched out on the leaf-soft ground.

They were in more settled country now and their progress would be increasingly slow. Barton was bone weary but it was two hours before sleep came to him. When he wakened the sun had left the canyon floor and its last rays bathed the high mountain crests in a crimson tide.

Cap was already sitting up, his back against the bole of a twisted tree, sucking morosely on his dead pipe.

Barton got tiredly to his feet, stretching to ease the stiffness of his muscles, then without a word went for the horses. There was no water in the little canyon, no food. They rode in hungry silence, each wrapped in his own thoughts. At a little after midnight they came upon the sorry buildings of a hill ranch and Barton put his animal into the yard without hesitation.

A dog rushed out at them, yammering with fierce defiance which died to a whining growl as they showed no intent of turning back. In the half-light of the thinning moon it stopped, a brown and yellow cur showing its coyote strain.

A voice from the house called in an uncertain note.

"Who is it?"

"Mitch Barton."

Almost at once a light was struck behind the window and a moment later a man appeared at the door. He wore long yellowed underwear and nothing more, and he cursed the cringing mongrel in a muffled undertone containing neither heat nor rancor, kicking at him with his bare foot as he came forward to where Barton had halted his horse.

"You, alive." He sounded incredulous. "There's a rumor around the valley that you're dead."

Barton said, "Only half," and swung wearily down. The man looked vaguely familiar and he realized suddenly that this was one of the Night Riders, but could not recall his name.

"How are things in the valley?"

"Terrible." The tone gained heat. "They haven't bothered us much up here yet, didn't know I'd ridden with you, but they're running out a lot of the people below."

He was leading them toward the house. A scrawny woman in a shapeless wrapper was already at the stove, coaxing the dying fire to new life, setting the coffeepot to boil and stirring up a bowl of batter cakes.

"We ain't got much"—the man's voice held no apology—"but what we have you're welcome to." He motioned them to the bench along the side of the rude table.

They ate gratefully, listening to the man's news, hearing more of the tight net thrown about Barton's ranch, and of the arrival of the State Guard. Kodyke, he thought, was again in the hills on his determined search for Barton.

Fed and rested they rode on and came before daylight to

the bench overlooking the valley where lay the ranch. It was the closest Barton had been to his home in over ten years and he dismounted, standing for a long while, looking down on the warmly remembered roll of land, on the buildings, miniature in the distance.

The horses were carefully hidden in a small draw and Cap stretched near them on the ground, his hat shielding his face from the growing light.

"Maybe now you'll tell me how you expect to get in there and get Marie and Ralph out alive."

"I don't."

Cap removed his hat and sat up. "You don't?"

"I don't expect to go in there, no. You're going in, while I pull the net apart."

Cap used his hook to scratch the side of his jaw. "Maybe I'm not thinking very clearly this morning."

Barton pointed down at the valley, at the golden tan grass tinged with pink, already beginning to summer cure, its ripening stems gleaming like waves where the small morning breeze ran through it. The precious grass that kept the ranch alive.

"What do you think they'll do when I set this to burning?"

Ayres looked down at the shining land. In the foothill country nothing was so badly feared as a grass fire.

Barton was saying levelly, "Let her get started and every man who can move, for miles around, will be up here trying to stop it."

Cap let his breath out slowly. "What if they don't stop it? What if it takes the buildings?"

Barton's sigh was deep, but no emotion told in his tone. "I'm not interested in the buildings, only in two people held there.

"As soon as the smoke is seen everybody down there will head here as fast as they can come. Maybe they'll leave one, maybe two guards. You'll have to handle the guards and get the Duchess and the boy. Then head for Nevada. I'll join you later if I can."

"What do you mean, if you can?"

Barton's face was drawn. "I want to make sure they don't put out the fire too soon, that they don't ride back in before you are clear . . ."

"Why don't I stay here and you go get them?"

Barton did not tell Cap that it took a man with two hands to accomplish what he intended. He meant to carry on a running fight, using the smoke from his fire for cover. He said merely, "Do what I ask, Cap. Catch an hour's sleep, then take Bell Canyon down. I'll give you two hours before I start the fire."

Ayres lay back, readjusting his hat, knowing by now that it was fruitless to argue with this man. He had the knack of turning off his mind, of relaxing utterly, and he was asleep within minutes.

The grass caught slowly. Barton had pulled a dozen handfuls and formed them into a small pile. He watched the bright flame lick upward, sending its tiny curl of smoke into the quiet air.

Then it went out. He crushed the pile flatter and tried a second match. This time it caught and he watched until the flames ate through the gathered pile. But again the fire died, for the grass was not fully dry.

The third time he nursed the flickering tongue carefully, hand-feeding it until it built heat enough to catch the surrounding grass, and then stepped back to watch the wall of fire build and spread and start to move, until the heat became so intense that the trees in its path burst and burned before the actual fire reached them.

Barton had the cattleman's loathing fear of fire on the range, and he saw the matted stems char and writhe and die with a sickness in his stomach. This was the winter's feed, curing on the ground. At this season of the year most of the herd had worked up into the higher meadows, but when the snow came they would drift back down, and this year there would be no food awaiting them.

Yet he could not worry about this now. It was a price he had to pay. He turned back up the draw and found his horse. The direction of the draft was down toward the ranch, but the wind might easily veer and he had no intention of allowing himself to become trapped.

He rode upward slowly, watching the fire as its arc widened, sweeping down the slope with greater and greater speed. Then, when the fire reached the flat land and the canyon was burned, when there was no longer the chance of his being caught by the flames, he reined the horse down, over the blackened, smoking earth.

The animal was skittish, not liking the smoke nor the crackling of the roaring fire, but he forced it on through the rising, acrid screen.

He heard the riders before he saw them, heard the sharp cries, the motion of their horses, and suddenly a man rode out of the smoke, a wraith appearing and becoming solid. Barton froze. The man was Kodyke.

They sat unmoving, staring at each other. Barton had believed Kodyke to be in the hills and the gunman on his part had heard no hint that Mitch was within miles of the ranch.

It was Kodyke who recovered first. His hand sped for his holstered gun and the movement released Barton. He swung his already triggered animal and drove him back into the shelter of the heavy smoke.

The bullet whistled by his head and a second shot tore into his saddle. Then he was in the pall and could hear Kodyke's high shout.

"It's Barton. Head him off."

There was a wild answer of yells as the riders forgot the fire and rushed in to intercept their prey. But Barton made no attempt to escape. He knew that if he attempted to ride on up the mountain they would be on his heels in an instant.

Instead, he circled, cutting through the fire, his horse jump-

THE NIGHT RIDERS / 143

ing convulsively as they crossed the line of flames. Here the smoke was denser; he could see less than fifty feet. Here a rider came out of the curtain and Barton threw a shot at him and saw the figure swerve away.

There were shots behind him, and a high yell as someone was hit, and a man cursing loudly.

"Watch it, damn you, it's me."

Barton's lips quirked with grim humor. He had an advantage which they did not possess. Anything that moved was his enemy while they were hampered by the possibility of hitting their friends.

The wind had freshened and the smoke billowed about him with choking force. He lifted his handkerchief, pulling it up to mask his nose and mouth, then he rode slowly eastward, his ears alert, his gun ready in his hand.

He came around a rock upthrust and jerked his animal to a sudden halt, for a rider had been waiting there.

The gun flashed almost in Barton's face, and the bullet struck his horse. The animal reared onto its hind legs, then toppled backward and Barton was thrown heavily to the rocky ground.

He rolled. He shot upward, lying on his side, and saw his adversary plunge from his seat and the frightened mount shy away to vanish in the whiteness around them.

He picked himself up slowly, walking forward, his finger still on the trigger, but the fallen man did not move. Barton bent down, feeling the wrist and finding no pulse. He had shot the man in the chest, just a little above the heart.

Straightening, he looked toward the fire and with a start realized his danger. It was less than thirty feet away. Mounted he had been able to maneuver, but on foot either the fire or his pursuers would reach him sooner or later. Sooner or later one of them would ride him down.

The dead man's rifle had fallen at his side. Barton reached for it, replacing his revolver in its holster, and then started walking quickly away from the fire. Below him was a swale, a depression some fifty feet across. He started down into it, the smoke blowing above him so that he could see clear across the declivity. Behind him the fire flared under a sudden thrust of wind that showered him with stinging sparks. One lit on his shoulder and burned through his shirt, making him jump. He beat it out, his attention diverted for the instant, and in that instant Kodyke dropped into the swale in front of him.

He brought up the rifle instinctively, firing even as Kodyke lifted his gun. The rifle bullet caught the man's wrist and sent the short gun spinning off to thud against a rock.

Kodyke sat in the saddle holding his burned wrist in his good hand, fully expecting death. Barton deliberately aimed at his breast. He pulled the trigger. Nothing happened. The rifle was empty.

With a muttered curse he threw it from him and clawed at the holstered revolver and Kodyke, seeing the action, raked his horse with his spurs, sending the animal lunging forward, rearing as it came.

One of the pawing front feet knocked Barton down backward and Kodyke followed, whether purposely or because he was thrown Barton did not know.

He only knew that the man was lying half-across him, struggling to get his gun. Barton knocked the hand away, pulled the gun and tried to press it against Kodyke's side.

The gunman caught Barton's arm, hauling it to him with wild strength, and sunk his teeth in above the wrist.

Barton rolled in a spasm of convulsive pain, flinging himself over and on top of Kodyke, wrenching at the wrist, but the mine policeman's jaw was clenched in a bulldog vice, and Barton rolled again.

Unable to fire, they fought in silence, Kodyke using his good hand to reach for Barton's face, to try to get his long fingers into Mitch's eyes, and Barton, wrestling, reached and reached again for the other's throat.

It was a test of strength as they strained against each other, neither conscious of the racing fire which had now reached the lip of the bowl.

Then Barton had a glimpse of the roiling flames beyond Kodyke and knew that he must break loose, that the fight must be finished. He put all of his strength into a thrust backward, hauling on the arm still clenched in Kodyke's teeth, and when the head lifted, Barton slammed it down again against the ground. He did not see the rock. He did not know that Kodyke's head struck it squarely, and that the skull cracked under the impact.

Kodyke died without sound and Barton dragged himself upright, staring around, rubbing vigorously at his bitten wrist. Then he turned and ran away from the advancing flames, struggling up the far lip of the swale, into the blowing smoke. The horseman almost rode him down.

Barton shot him, feeling the pain shoot through his arm as he pulled the trigger, and with his other hand grabbed the horse's bridle as the animal pivoted away. The horse almost dragged him from his feet but he steadied it, then led it back to where the rider lay. The man was dead.

Mitch Barton mounted and headed south, out of the smoke, riding as he had never ridden before.

CHAPTER TWENTY

Cap Ayres circled the ranch twice before he ventured down into the big, bare yard. When he did ride in his gun was in his hand, the reins neatly held by the gleaming hook.

The first man he saw was Finley Barton. He came out of the blacksmith shop and stopped, his eyes going wide with startled shock. Then he turned and would have run back inside but Cap's gun jerked and the bullet caught Finley in the shoulder, spinning him around and dropping him in the doorway.

146 / THE NIGHT RIDERS

Cap climbed down and walked forward to bend down and turn the figure over.

"Where are they?"

There had been a second man in the blacksmith shop. He came out suddenly, an iron bar raised above his head. Cap saw the movement from one corner of his eye. He swung and fired and missed, and the bar crashed down on his good arm, splintering the bone.

The man stepped in then, confident that he had won, swinging the bar again, at Cap's head. Cap ducked the blow and his hook lashed out in a curving sweep which reached the man's shoulder, knifing through it, stripping the flesh away.

The bar dropped, the man grabbed his shoulder and ran shrieking across the yard. It was the scream which brought Marie Beauchamp to the door of the small building where she and the boy had been held prisoner.

She saw Ayres and, calling his name, ran down the hill. Ralph Barton followed, and they found Cap leaning against the wall of the shop, the pain from his broken arm making him dizzy.

"How many more are there around?" Cap asked.

"I don't know."

"Get my gun."

She obeyed.

"All right, let's have a look in the house."

"Where's Mitch?"

"At the fire." He looked away, at the distant swell of smoke, then moved to the house with her beside him, the boy behind them.

There was no one in the building. They came out again to see Finley Barton dragging himself to his feet. Cap walked at him, swinging the hook suggestively.

"Can you saddle horses with one hand?"

Barton's cousin stared at them sullenly. "My shoulder is broken."

Cap said without humor, "You've still got one hand." He looked at the Duchess. "I guess it's up to you."

"Not until I take care of this arm of yours."

"Never mind that." Cap's tone was rough. "We've got to clear out of here." He moved unsteadily to the corral fence, cursing the Confederate ball which had carried away his hand at Gettysburg.

The hardest thing was to catch the horses. Finley flatly refused to help. The hook was useless in throwing a rope and Marie Beauchamp simply could not master the casting of a loop. The horses, wise in the ways of men, circled fluidly, keeping just out of reach.

They were still trying to catch them when Barton rode in. His appearance brought a quick call of dismay from Marie Beauchamp. His eyebrows had been singed to invisibility beneath the smoke and grime on his face, and his coat and shirt held a dozen holes.

"Mitch!"

He swung down to hold her in his arms, her body trembling against him in the excess of her relief.

"Oh, Mitch."

He was staring across her shoulder at Cap's dangling arm. "What did they do to you?"

Ayres told him in a dozen words.

Barton nodded. "Let's get going. Some of the men may come back any time."

"Kodyke?"

"Dead." Barton picked up the rope the Duchess had dropped and stepped quickly into the corral. He roped one horse and another and a third, leading them outside and fastening them to the fence. Then he threw on the saddles.

Finley had sat down weakly in the shade of one of the sheds. "You're not going to leave me? I gotta get to a doctor," he said plaintively.

Barton paid him no attention. He lifted the boy onto one of

the horses, helped the Duchess mount, then boosted Cap into a saddle and looped the reins over the hook.

"Can you make it?"

Ayres said, "Sure. You and Marie and Ralph cut out. I'll ride for the Ferry and let Doc Wilson glue this arm back together." Even as he spoke he swayed in the saddle.

"We'll all ride for the Ferry. With Kodyke dead no one is going to bother Marie or Ralph."

"What about you?"

"I'm not going to stay in the Ferry. I've got something else to do."

He swung into the saddle ahead of the boy and rode beside Ayres, out of the yard, pausing as he passed the gate. The smoke from the grass fire looked a great deal closer and the wind was already dropping cinders around them.

The buildings would go. There was no saving them now, but they had served their purpose. He rode on. The buildings did not matter, nothing mattered except that the Duchess and Ralph were safe.

Doc Wilson was at home, working quietly in his garden. He showed no surprise at sight of them. Barton wondered if anything in the world could any longer surprise the man.

Wilson helped Cap into the house. He cut away the sleeve and made a tish-tishing sound when he saw the jagged end of the broken bone pressing through the shredded skin.

It took Barton's help to set the arm and neither spoke until the splints were lashed in place. Cap had fainted from the pain. He lay quietly on the bed, looking curiously old, curiously shrunken.

They went quietly from the room then. In the hall Barton said, "Can I leave Marie and the boy here? Ask Cap to take care of them if anything happens to me."

"Where are you going?"

The Duchess also came from the bedroom. Barton turned, took her shoulders and pulled her against him gently, but made no attempt to kiss her.

"I'm going after Kruger."

She drew away from him. "Mitch, no. You'll be killed."

He said, "Maybe, but probably not. I'll be careful."

"But you'll kill him."

"If I can. Killing Hague and Kodyke is not enough. That's merely lopping off the branches of an evil tree. As long as Kruger lives the battle is not finished. He deserves to die."

She said tensely, "I wasn't thinking about him, but about you. You've killed before, but always in an open fight, in fairness. This is the first time you've set out deliberately to murder a man."

He was silent.

"Don't elect yourself an executioner. You will have to live with it all of your life. Haven't you done enough? You can go away, to Canada, to Mexico, anywhere. I'll go with you."

Still he did not answer. He looked at her for a long moment and then swung quickly to the door.

CHAPTER TWENTY-ONE

DONALD KRUGER SAT AT HIS DESK staring in disbelief at the man who had slipped in and dared to sit down in the opposing chair, and the tide of anger came up through him in a torrent such as he had never before experienced.

Carl Dill was saying calmly, "I did your dirty chores for a long time, Kruger, and what thanks did I get? Five years in prison."

Kruger did not even try to answer.

Dill went on, savoring now what he had to say. No one had tried to bar his entry, no one had questioned his right to be here, and wanted man though he was he was safe here with this empire builder, safe because of what he knew.

"I just wanted to tell you that it was I who arranged Barton's escape, I who stirred the valley up against you enough to make them wreck the mine."

Kruger tried to speak and found that he could not. And Dill continued boring.

"And it was I who brought on your final ruin. No one thought to check the bank's cash reserve, no one but me. I had two friends check this morning. I've sent messages to the banking board, to your correspondent boards, to a dozen of your biggest depositors. When you open your doors in the morning there will be a run, a run which will set off a panic on the Exchange.

"You're through, Donald Kruger. There is no way to save yourself. Think about that, when the prison doors close on you. Think about Carl Dill then."

Kruger knew Dill's type too well to hope that the man was lying, and he was fully aware of the financial tightrope he had been walking since the closing of the mines. He had not the slightest doubt that the merest whisper of suspicion would start a run that the bank could not possibly weather.

He got up slowly. His face had a gray tinge and his eyes widened and bulged. Still Dill was not afraid, only pleased with himself as Kruger moved like a sleepwalker around the desk, around to stand behind the seated man.

"I am going to kill you."

Dill spun then, thoroughly startled, and looked up into the eyes of a Kruger he had never seen before. There was a paralyzing terror in the very control the mining man exercised, far more frightening than if he had ranted or cursed. Dill tried to push his chair back against the deep carpet.

"Now, wait . . ."

Kruger's hand were already reaching for his throat. They were big hands, strengthened by the early days of his own mining and powerful still, and directed now by a purpose blinding in its intensity.

Dill suddenly tried to fight back, tried to tear the strangling fingers from his throat. He could not move them. The breath

THE NIGHT RIDERS / 151

went out of him. His face turned purple, his tongue began to protrude, and at last he slumped back in his chair.

Even then Kruger did not release his grip. He was a thorough man, meticulous by instinct even in murder. It was not until he was certain that no life remained in the struggling, then limp body that he opened his hands and let the dead thing fall to the floor. Without looking at it he turned away to gather up a handful of papers from the huge carved desk.

With these in his grasp he straightened his coat and headed for the door, as unperturbed as if he were going to a board meeting. He stopped once before leaving the room to look back. It was incomprehensible that this small, unimportant creature had actually brought about his ruin.

He had never had any respect for Dill, for what he was or what he stood for. To Kruger the man had been but a cog in the machine he had been building, and when that cog had proved defective he had sent Dill to prison and forgot him, never expecting to see him again.

Kruger came out into the main foyer of the bank and paused to look up, around the cathedral-sized room. It was after hours. The massive doors giving on Montgomery Street were closed and locked, but inside the tellers and cashiers still labored behind their wickets, posting the entries for the day.

He stood as was his custom, admiring the grandeur and spaciousness of the place. No bank in North America, perhaps in the world, was more imposing. He had poured money into the building as he had poured it into so many other buildings in his beloved San Francisco. This town was his. He had been midwife to all its growing life.

He spoke to no one as he traveled the distance to the small side door where the private guard ushered him out and locked the panel behind him.

He stopped in the sunlit street, deeply inhaling the salt air from the Bay and the mingling odors which had a thousand origins, the perfume brought to his city from all of the earth's surface. Empty now, tomorrow morning this sidewalk would

152 / THE NIGHT RIDERS

be crowded with people fighting, struggling to get into the bank, to recover their savings, which were already lost.

Yet to Kruger they were not lost. Ruthlessly he had torn silver from Nevada, gold from the California hills not for himself but to enrich, to embellish, to beautify and make great the city he loved. And like many a king in love, he had ruined his land to serve his beloved.

He walked in reverie to the carriage which waited at the curb and did not speak to the coachman who helped him in, and honoring his master's withdrawal the coachman turned down through the Mission and on toward the Peninsula.

Mitchell Barton saw them coming a long way off, the carriage moving slowly as if the man within was prolonging this trip as much as possible. They turned through the gates and Barton watched them from his place of concealment, tempted to step out and have the showdown now but containing his impatience.

Half a dozen laborers were scattered around the great grounds, still working in the afternoon sun. Barton waited almost an hour before they gathered their tools and disappeared, then he moved up the driveway and mounted the steps to the two-storied, pillared porch of the Monterey-style mansion. A houseman answered his knock and he asked for Kruger.

The man shook his head. "He gave absolute orders that he was not to be disturbed by anyone."

"He'll see me," Barton said, and drew his gun.

The servant drew his breath in audible fright.

"Where is he?"

The man said through stiff lips, "In his study."

"Show me."

They crossed the high, square hall with its wood paneling and imported Italian furniture, and paused before the heavy double doors. The servant knocked and Kruger's voice reached them faintly.

"I told you I do not want to be disturbed."

THE NIGHT RIDERS / 153

The houseman's voice shook. "I know, sir, but there's a man here to see you. It's very important." His eyes held on Barton's gun.

"Who is he?"

"Mitchell Barton." The voice was loud enough, but there was no feeling in his tone.

There was a short pause, then Kruger's voice again, in a falling note. "You're too late, Barton. Dill came ahead of you."

"Dill?"

The answer came lower, almost muffled. "He's dead in my office. I killed him." There was a silence in the study, and Barton put his hand upon the ornate knob.

Before he could turn it there was the quick, sharp report of a single shot.

For an instant Barton thought that Kruger was firing at him through the door, then, as no second report came, as there was no sign of a hole in the smooth panel, he yelled at the terrified servant.

"Get out of the way."

The man sidestepped as Barton backed, then hit the doors with his shoulder. The center lock snapped and the doors were flung inward, crashing against the walls on either side.

Donald Kruger lay beside the desk, vermilion from the hole in his temple already staining the carpet beneath him and the gun near his body giving up its wisps of powder smoke.

Barton stopped in mid-stride, letting his own weapon drop to his side. He stood for a long moment looking down on the man he had hated for so long, then he moved around the desk, drawn by the sheet of white paper, the note Kruger had left there.

It was addressed to the Governor of California, and it was long. Barton picked it up, sketching through it. Kruger had deliberately pulled down the house of cards which had been his empire.

Here were recounted all of his machinations, not boastfully, but factually as a banker would present it, exactly what he had done, the names of his associates, the names of the legislators who had been on his payroll, the judges and law-enforcement officers who had been responsible for the trials of the Night Riders ten years earlier.

Barton found his own name there along with those who had gone to prison with him. He stopped reading then. He turned. The paralyzed servant was still motionless in the doorway.

"Call the police now, and tell them exactly what happened," Barton said quietly.

The man came alive, his eyes widened. "You aren't going to be here?"

Barton shook his head. "I'm going to Sacramento to see the governor. Then I'm going back to Morgan's Ferry. Tell the police that. If they want my testimony they can find me there . . . and I hope I never have to leave the valley again."

He looked down again at the dead man. Kruger had nearly ruined his life, had all but ruined the valley in his hunger for gold. Yet before taking his life he had made this gesture toward amends. It was entirely out of character, and suddenly Barton understood. Kruger who had never shown more than ruthless selfishness had never labored for himself, but always to create a dream, to build a city, and his animosities had been only for the things that stood in his way.

It would be something to tell the Yankee Duchess, to try to get across to his growing son who would hear the distorted stories as time built its web of folklore.

There would be those who would revere Kruger's memory and those who would curse him for a fiend. It would be Barton's lifelong job to remember, to repeat, that the man he had fought had had a worthy dream, that his blunder, his blindness that had brought him down, had been in forgetting the stature of man.